TUESDAY AT THREE

TUESDAY AT THREE

GILLIAN ALEX

ARCHWAY
PUBLISHING

Cover Design by
Marcus Marritt, www.marcusmarrittillustrator.com

Editing and Typography by
Kate E. Stephenson, www.KempsConsulting.com

Archway Publishing books may be ordered
through booksellers or by contacting:

Archway Publishing
1663 Liberty Drive
Bloomington, IN 47403
www.archwaypublishing.com
1 (888) 242-5904

ISBN: 978-1-4808-3422-4 (sc)
ISBN: 978-1-4808-3423-1 (e)

Library of Congress Control Number: 2016911220

Print information available on the last page.

Archway Publishing rev. date: 11/10/2016

This book is dedicated to Shirley, Darrell, and Gwen.

This book is dedicated to my aunts Ecki and Brenda.

This book is dedicated to my twelve best friends.

This book is dedicated to my editor, Kate.

This book is dedicated to every person who has ever come up to me on the street, in a store, or the airport and told me that they liked my hair.

This book is dedicated to every only child who isn't afraid to talk to themselves.

This book is dedicated to every boy who didn't support my dreams, didn't see me after the first date, or who I dated long term but never wanted to marry me, and I thank you soo much for the lack of effort on your part because if you had the balls to propose, right now, the only thing I would be is your stupid wife.

This book is dedicated to me...

CONTENTS

JANUARY

Sunday, January 1, 2012
12:00am
Happy New Year! Not soo much…

Monday, January 2nd
12:01am
It's been twenty-four hours and the stroke of midnight hasn't made a bit of difference. Amidst all of the confetti and streamers, champagne, and smiling faces, I'm still hurting. The "ball drop" didn't mean shit. Hell, if I never see another New Year's Eve again, it will be too soon. Steven was never going to give me what I wanted. I asked. I begged. I cried. I just wanted to get married, but he didn't and as much as I want to hate him, I can't.

4:30pm
Been thinking all day. I probably need to see a shrink, but would much rather spend the money on a great dinner with friends or a pair of pricey pretty pumps. So instead, after I hit the gym, I'm stopping at Papyrus and picking up a journal. This will be my therapy. I will chronicle my true feelings. My office always winds down midday and the minute I see an open window, I will stop and write.
Let's see if this works…

Tuesday, January 3rd
1:15pm
Today is perfect. The office is dead. My boss, Joan, is on holiday and I don't need to be back to the office until Friday. I only came in to sign for a package from FEDEX and then I'm outta here, but not before I pull out my journal and write. My heart is heavy. This will be my first entry.

Journal Entry #1

"Love of My Life"

I've already met him. We are not married. We are not dating. We are not a couple, but I am in love with him and he is in love with me. I respect him so much that I will not tell his secrets and only give my friends tidbits of our escapades. He is my rock. He is the boy version of me strong, caring, and humble. He completes me. I am his favorite and he is my everything. We get each other and respect what we have. Truthfully, we could care less about the sordid details of each other's lives. So I don't care where he spends his weekends; he doesn't care who gave me my latest bauble; and neither one of us cares to discuss who we are sleeping with. We cherish our memories and live the time we still spend together like it is endless. Anything outside of us is meaningless.

What we have is not complicated as there is no one object, one place, or one time in our lives that our friendship is built on. I didn't stop falling in love with him when the gifts stopped. He didn't stop missing me because we couldn't talk. He holds the key to my heart and he knows it. He is the one who I don't have to hold my breath for when we are together because his only wish is that I breathe. I don't have to long for his touch because it's always there. When we are together, women are jealous and men are mesmerized. We are a power couple, a good guy and a great girl.

Break-ups have a way of showing you both the good and bad about yourself. I now realize that the love of my life is not the guy who had me at hello — instead; he is the guy that still has me at good-bye. I only hope that I will meet him again.

Friday, January 6ᵗʰ

7:00am
After five days of self-evaluation, tears, and vodka —
I'M BACK and it's official. I'm ready to take on the New
Year and all SHE has to offer.

8:15am
On the way to the office and the subway train is
packed. A businessman carrying an attaché case in one
hand and the *Wall Street Journal* in the other just
yelled at me to "MOVE IN." Only in New York City.

9:00am
Miraculously, there is no line at the deli on East
41ˢᵗ. I'm ordering egg whites and turkey bacon on wheat
toast with coffee. All for $3.50 — cheapest breakfast
in America.

10:01am
The office is still dead.

12:00pm
Joan sent an email; she's expecting another package.
As soon as it arrives I'm outta here.

3:00pm
Finally! The package arrived and now it's yoga time.
Class starts at four o'clock, so I'll make it in plenty
of time.

6:00pm
Leaving yoga. Bikram Yoga (hot yoga) is set up in three
rows in front of a mirror so you can see everybody.
Now the practice calls for you to be one with yourself
while the heat works to cleanse both your mind and
body of toxins, except I was watching *him* which
was making me the other kind of hot. The guy who
was in front of me during class is a Black Matthew
McConaughey, both rugged and sexy. I was staring at
him the whole time. I would have licked the sweat off

his back. Yeah — he is *that* fine. And he invited me to dinner next week.

On the elevator ride down, Mr. BMM introduced himself and gave me his card:

Darren Blake
Blake Capital LLC
CEO

6:15pm
I need a snack so I'm stopping at Gray's Papaya to get a hot dog. I know this is bad, but that's why I work out; so I can eat like a pig and drink like a fish.

7:00pm
Last minute invite from my girlfriend, Ava. She wants me to meet her at a restaurant in midtown. Tonight's dinner is courtesy of Levine, Thurman & Rowe. She just made partner. She's a POWER bitch and she's expensing it.

8:00pm
Heading back downtown. I did the transformation in record time.

9:59pm
Dinner was great and we're going to keep the party going, but I need to hit the bathroom to fix my face.

10:09pm
Still in the bathroom and now chatting up the chick at the sink next to me. We exchange compliments. I gushed over her belt and shoes while she praised my ring and bracelet. As we continue to bond over the importance of accessorizing, I tell her my name, Alexa. She tells me hers, Kelly. She then asks, "What's your story?" I tell her the truth: I work as an executive assistant, but run a small accessory company. She smiles and hands me her card, telling me to give her a call. As luck would have it, she works for *Accessory Magazine*. This is huge.

11:15pm
Ava and I just made it to a lounge in midtown and the
stares can't stop.

11:20pm
A casually dressed older white guy is coming our
way and he is all smiles. When he approaches, he
introduces himself as the owner. His name is Liam.
Of course he asks what we are drinking and as Ava
hesitates, I jump right in enthusiastically stating,
"Two martinis, dirty with olives."

Saturday, January 7th
12:21am
Fast forward. We are on round three and Ava has
loosened up and is now the one doing all the talking.
We are having fun.

2:30am
Liam had his driver take us home and since I live
uptown, I'm the last stop.

2:44am
My feet are on FIRE! and I can barely make it up the
last flight of stairs to my apartment. As soon as I get
to the door of my apartment, I'm kicking my pumps off.

2:49am
I'm in and as my feet regain consciousness, my phone
buzzes. It's a text from my lover, Kola.
                    I MISS U BABY...WHERE R U

1:16am
My reply: JUST GOT IN. CUM OVER.

3:00am
My Kola. He's sleep. I'm staring at him. He's twenty-
seven, African, and an amazing lover. He's the third
African guy I've been with. My first was from Senegal,
second Mali, and Kola is from Nigeria. Now based on

what some may view as only minimal experience, my belief is that all African men are granted access to the States if and only if they pass a love making test. Further, unlike my previous lovers, Kola was born here proving that this trait can be inherited and passed down from generation to generation. *My God...*

Sunday, January 8th
2:30pm
Day Party!! I'm on my way to the Meat Packing District to meet the girls for Sunday Brunch. Ava, Madelyn, and Cindy. They are my jury. My partners in crime. My friends.

4:02 pm
Our table is flooded with Italian heartthrobs and I'm holding on to every other word from the sexiest. His name is GianMarco and I can barely understand him but who cares. He's a sweetheart. Not only do we exchange numbers, but he gives me cab fare and then says: *"Pereme non vai a Casa? Cosi ti puoi riposare. Ci vediamo fiv tardi."* I look at him and smile. He gently kisses my cheek and begins to translate. He wants me to go home and rest my head and promises that when he returns to the States we'll hang out. Now until then, I'm jumping on the train and using my cab money for a mani/pedi. The first book I read when I moved to New York City was *Coffee, Tea or Me?* (circa 1968) and let's just say that the game ain't changed.

Monday, January 9th
7:30pm
Exhausted from my action packed weekend, but today's saving grace was that Joan was working from home so the day breezed by.

Didn't have to do shit and now I'm on the way to meet BMM from the yoga class. I swore I was going to stop with all of the snooping and *Dateline* investigations antics when I meet a new guy, but I must have someone in the office run a D&B report on Blake Capital LLC.

10:15pm
My date tonight was nice and I'm looking forward to hanging out with BMM again. Yes, that's his official nickname. My girlfriends and I always give guys a nickname. Not only do we find them hilarious as usually they are a spot-on description, for better or worse; but they serve as a means for us to discuss the guy sometimes right in his presence and him not even know it.

11:00pm
I'm home and I really want to pull out my journal and write. It felt soo good last week, but I'm actually going to wait until tomorrow afternoon. There's something about taking a break during the day that I like. It's like my adult version of a "time out".

Tuesday, January 10th
12:05pm
I'm outta here on Joan's heels. She just left for a business lunch and I'm timing this escape like a movie script. I'm guessing she will stop at the bathroom and then three minutes later will be pressing the down button on the elevator. That gives me five minutes until my exit. I'm going to a business lunch of sorts myself. Hitting the Mediterranean restaurant around the corner. I'm ordering the prefix, a glass of wine and bringing my journal. I'm going to pretend that I'm a writer.

Journal Entry #2

"I Love New York"

Yesterday when I exited the subway, I received a text message from BMM stating that he was running about thirty minutes late for our date. That was perfect because, as usual, I was running twenty minutes late. We were meeting in Union Square so, rather than change my shoes one block away from the restaurant like I usually do, I decided to brave the three blocks in my heels. As I was sitting on a bench about to do the "switch-out" from my TB flats to my wedges, a girl sat down next to me and, before I even had the chance to compliment her nail polish, she tackled her own "switch-out" from Manolos to ballerina flats and, pulling out a cigarette and lighter, collapsed back on the bench. As this whole transaction was going down all I could think to myself was:

This is why I Love NYC...

It seems like it is the only place in the world where girls really own their WOMANHOOD. We practice it daily and parade it around triumphantly. We gracefully march around the city like we own it. Women move through New York City like lightning. We carry some of the best bags, filled with everything from gym clothes and makeup to textbooks and laptops.

Chicks in New York City know how to find their lane and stay in it. We breeze past movie sets with an attitude and can't be bothered by the cavalcade of construction workers' catcalls. The hustle and bustle of the city turns us into straight shooters.

We either like you or we don't. We party Uptown or Downtown. We're in love with the Lower Eastside or detest the Upper Westside.

The opportunities for success here are endless. You can land a job at the company of your dreams and work your way up or simply work any ol' day job as long as it gives you the freedom to pursue your true passion.

It's the one city where you do not judge a book by its cover — if only because you are likely to be standing next to a millionaire on the subway or cycling next to a politician in Spin class. It's the one city where knowing the bouncer at a lounge is more important than knowing the owner of the lounge.

Sometimes it's hard to concentrate with all the adventure that's waiting at your doorstep. It's a grown woman's playground and, if you have the right toys, you're happy to skip naptime.

Although I'm a California girl and credit my cool, laid-back upbringing for my cheerful demeanor, I'm glad that I ended up here. This city continues to prove its loyalty to me by way of great restaurants, great people and great fun.

Thursday, January 11ᵗʰ
9:00am
Just got to the office. Joan is out until Friday hosting an offsite meeting. *Hallelujah*! That being said, I'm going to make good use of the extra time by doing two-a-days at the gym, sending emails out to boutiques, and sourcing new places to get materials. I sent Kelly from *Accessory Magazine* an email and want to be prepared when she replies.

Friday, January 13ᵗʰ
2:03pm
Kola called. He wants to take me out on a date this weekend. SHOCKING! This will be a first. We met last fall at a party and, so far, it's only been a late night/early morning kind of thing for us.

3:15pm
BMM called. He wants to go out again when he returns from his business trip abroad. He said he enjoyed our date and is looking forward to us spending more time together. I smiled when our call ended. I like him.

5:00pm
Michael called. He's been off the radar for some time now. I met him two summers ago at a rooftop party. He's rich. He's white. Early forties and a full prick. I only tolerate him because he takes me to great restaurants and the hottest lounges. I won't throw him completely under the bus, because I too am a bit of a show off and foodie and, at times, I can be shallow. He said he's been thinking about me, but is working on a huge project. He wants us to hang as soon as his schedule frees up.

5:02pm
I just realized today is "Friday the 13ᵗʰ." A day that is supposed to be taboo, but based off of all the phone calls and invitations I've received thus far, maybe the 13ᵗʰ is my new lucky day.

Sunday January 15ᵗʰ
6:00pm
Just hung up with Kola. Our phone call was quick. I'm getting a mani/pedi and he was on the way to get a haircut. He said tonight would be a "date night" and to look pretty.

11:59pm
Kola just sent a text:
> SUP LEX? MEET ME AT FLOTUS.
> B THERE @ 1:00.

Monday, January 16ᵗʰ
12:10am
My reply: OK

4:03am
Great night. Never made it to Flotus. Got dressed and met Madelyn at a lounge in Soho. I understand this is NYC and there is no specific time that a date should start or end, but Kola should have started planning our date way before that stroke of midnight.

Tuesday, January 17ᵗʰ
3:15pm
Ay dios mio. I'm actually busy today. I didn't even have time to hit 'Bucks. Tim, one of Joan's directs, is a pain in my ass. He's useless. I swear he needs directions on how to hold his dick and take a piss.

4:00pm
Finally. Tim's gone and I can take a break. I'm dipping into a conference room and writing in my journal.

Journal Entry #3

"Girls Rule the World"

On the way home last night, I was in the back of the cab listening to the Nas Billboard hit "If I Ruled the World" featuring Lauryn Hill. The cab driver was peering at me through the rearview mirror and as I gently bobbed my head to the beat I let out a soft smile. Because I know that I am a WOMAN and, in fact, it is us who rule the world.

We are a far better and stronger breed. We are most definitely the greatest beings to walk the Earth, leaving us with only one rival who shares our strength and determination – the female cockroach. Why?? Because she usually shows up uninvited and doesn't care, she can go for a month without eating, and she doesn't need a male to reproduce.

She is our only true competition.

Wednesday, January 18th
6:00am
I'm leaving a message for Joan. I'm calling in sick today. I don't want to go to the office and when I return tomorrow, my plan for the rest of the week is to do nothing.

Thursday, January 19th
9:00am
Stopping at Starbucks for a Tall Extra Hot Skinny Vanilla Cappuccino.

9:15am
Made it to the office. Pushed papers around on my desk to appear busy.

5:15pm
Leaving office. Going home to do nothing.

Friday, January 20th
9:00am
Made it to the office. Grabbed folders from the supply room.

9:15am
I need 'Bucks. Espresso here I come.

9:35am
Spreading the folders around on my desk to appear busy.

5:15pm
Leaving office. Going home to do nothing.

Saturday, January 21st
I did nothing. Didn't even go to Starbucks. Didn't even go to the gym.

Monday, January 23ʳᵈ
11:33pm
Still nothing... It's clear as much as I want to believe my own hype I'm nowhere near close to my testament of "I'M BACK" that I preached a few weeks ago. Instead *I'm back* — to self doubt, to feeling hurt, to feeling sad.

Tuesday, January 24ᵗʰ
6:00pm
At a dive bar by myself drowning my sorrows with cheap happy hour margaritas. There are two guys to my left talking about their wives and an older gentleman to my right who is quite dapper. He's either the owner or this place is his local hangout. I have my journal in my bag and I'm going to sit right here at the bar and write.

Journal Entry #4

"News Flash! My Life"

A single girl in NYC can come to the Upper West Side and be reminded of the fact that she **doesn't** have a husband and baby or go to the Upper East Side and be reminded that she **doesn't** have a Birkin Bag. Some days Life Fucking Sucks. I mean, is this where my life is headed right now? I'm thirty, not married, and have no kids, but I think I'm happy. I mean I love myself and I love life. It's strange though because I know I want more. I have always been very independent and romantically optimistic that my perfect guy is out there. But sometimes even the preacher prays for worshippers. We all reach a point in our lives when we begin to doubt ourselves and the decisions we've made. I am beginning to think I have made some wrong decisions.

There is no questioning the fact that I am my own biggest fan. After all, if you can't cheer for yourself then who will cheer for you? But even the cheerleader longs to be able to go home with the quarterback — so where the hell is my Eli Manning, Robert Griffin, Tom Brady?

Physically I look great, although I'm constantly breaking my diet.

Spiritually I'm okay, but I always have a hangover on Sunday mornings so I could never fully commit to attending church services regularly.

Financially I'm sort of a wreck as I've broken Suze Orman's golden rule and am using my 401K like a pot of gold.

Sexually I'm at an all-time high!! I know how to satisfy myself and know without a doubt I'm a great lover.

But...

Romantically I'm suffering.

To date, NY has produced not one single person that I long for. No one single guy that's made my heart stop. No one person whose voice I feel like I need to hear everyday. I have never confessed to anybody how romantically lonely I feel. I miss having a steady guy in my life. Not one that I have to take a plane to go visit and try to get thirty days' worth of couple's stuff shoved into five, but one who lives in the same city as me and who can see me every day. One who will come over to my apartment if I call and tell him I saw a mouse or that I'm afraid of thunder. Really I just want someone to tell me that he loves me. I miss hearing those three words. I really miss it. It has been soo long since I've heard those words from the lips of someone I adore. I just want to be loved. I want to know just by someone's touch that they missed me...

Oh Lord... Tears are in my eyes — it must be time for a drink...

Wednesday, January 25ᵗʰ

5:00am

I'm lying in my bed, wide awake. I wish I could turn my mind off. It's going a mile a minute as I recount every move I've made over the past five years. Before deciding to move, I visited every Fashion Week for a year and half and after seeing my tenth show, I was hooked. One of my dearest friends Marie hooked me up with one of her college friends who works in PR. She invited me to great events and introduced me to all the right people. She even let me crash on her couch before I got my own place. You see, in my mind **everything** was going to change as soon as I got my own apartment and my big break. At last, I would have: my solid career, my perfect guy, and a happy home. And as I turn over, close my eyes and clinch my pillow; it's clear that working to achieve everything is going to take EVERYTHING.

7:30am

Just woke up a new woman. I'm not sure who this chick is, but I'm going to do my best to try and figure HER out.

3:00pm

Kelly replied to my email! I'm excited. Her magazine is having a small pre-Fashion Week party and she has extended an invitation that I can't turn down. They are doing a gift bag and she needs twenty-five pieces. I'm excited. I need this.

I must admit that I'm losing my passion for design. Maybe this is Mother Earth's way of giving me my last hooray at this business. As worldly as I believe I am, a small piece of me is highly spiritual which leaves me open to the possibilities of the unknown. Deep down inside I feel like some other door is slowly opening and inviting me in.

7:00pm

Ooh BMM... We had an amazing phone call. It may have had something to do with him being a little tipsy but

I was buying everything he was selling so I really don't care. He's in London and there is a six hour time difference. He's returned from a night out with clients. We spoke for thirty minutes and I let him do most of the talking. He made several promises during our phone call and my hope is that he keeps them.

Friday, January 27th
8:00 pm
At home working. Feathers and flowers are all over the floor in the living room. I'm making barrettes. Silk flower petals, Swarovski crystals and feather accents. They are very Carrie Bradshaw. No doubt her character had amazing style, but it was the details that we all fell in love with. Her accessories – her shoes, her bags, her cute mole, and her undying devotion to Mr. Big. Just ask any stylist from Rachel Zoe to June Ambrose, a smart, stylish girl's life is built on her accessories.

Saturday, January 28th
10:00am
I live uptown in Washington Heights so instead of my usual Starbucks run, I'm going to hit the block and grab *cafe con leche y azúcar* – a neighborhood fave.

2:01pm
Working on the barrettes. I just put the finishing touches on #14.

5:30pm
Taking a nap. My bedroom is a shitty-ass mess. Feathers, clothes, shoes – they are everywhere.

11:00pm
Exhausted. Just getting in from the gym. When I flick on the light in the kitchen I'm reminded of my *not so* strict work ethic. The counter is littered with empty wine bottles. I drop my bag and open the fridge to retrieve yet another one. I grab a glass from the cupboard and laugh aloud as I begin to pour because

20

I often rely on a lil' happy juice to get my creative juices flowing and so far this practice has paid off.

Sunday, January 29th
5:30pm
Taking a break. Not only are my hands cramping, but I've stuck myself with pins too many times to count and have almost singed my fingertips off with the glue gun. I feel bad for my upstairs neighbors. I have consistently been dropping the *f-bomb* for three days straight and I know they can hear me.

10:31pm
Kola sent a text. I'm ignoring it. I really want to answer but I must stay focused.

Monday, January 30th
12:00am
Yay! I'm done. Twenty-five beautiful barrettes are ready. They are neatly lined up in rows of five on my small living room table and then my glass coffee table. My label — **aLexaRoss** — is neatly placed on the back. I wrap the last barrette and place it in the box and smile. This business brought me to New York. Sure, the move was coupled with heartache and fear, but I'm here and I'm grateful.

Tuesday, January 31st
8:05am
Power Failure! Joan sent a text to **STAY HOME.** There's an electrical problem in the building.

10:05am
WAKE AND BAKE... I sent Kola a text. He's on his way. He is a big weed head and today I'm joining him.

1:15pm
Kola and I finished brunch. I made cheese eggs smothered potatoes and bacon. He's napping and I'm going to write.

Journal Entry #5

"Apartment 46"

My mother always said that at some point in a woman's life, she should live by herself. I never really understood what she meant until I got my own place in NYC. Although I had the best of times with my prior roommates, living by myself offers a new freedom. Every day when I come home I am free to explore my wants, ideas, feelings, and desires. No one is there to stand in my way.

Simply stated: You can play with your hair or play with your pussy with no interruptions.

Living by yourself offers solace — true solace that can only be achieved in your own space. You can hear your voice or you can experience utter silence. You can have true quiet time, a time when you can hear only your thoughts. This silence allows you to have passion. Passion with yourself. A feeling of "Honey, I'm home" — but instead of making an announcement, you make a statement by just being. It is okay to be alone sometimes; it's okay to be "okay" with yourself.

Knowing that you can come in, drop your bags, kick off your sneakers at the front door and not to worry about moving them — that's stellar. The freedom of going into the bathroom, peeling off your clothes to shower, and leaving your panties on the floor. Cooking while you are naked and being able to scratch your ass, knowing that no one is watching.

We all enjoy good company, but learning to enjoy your own is important. Actually, it's monumental.

No, I'm wrong — it's EVERYTHING.

FEBRUARY

Wednesday, February 1st
11:00am
I'm sitting at my desk thinking: I need a new boy and when I say BOY, I mean just that.

Translation:
I'm a **girl** – PINK, and I need a **boy** – BLUE.

People always try to rag on me because I use those terms, but I believe that at the end of the day, we are actually that simple.

Girls = PINK: soft, full of emotion, hope, glee
Boys = BLUE: steady, resourceful, guarded

We are different creatures and everyday I'm slowly figuring that out.

Thursday, February 2nd
10:45am
Joan is on my ass this morning. I'm busy. She needs travel booked, meetings set up, and personal appointments scheduled. Note: she's a Bergdorf Blonde and that is the "one appointment" I can't screw up.

11:35am
Finally. Starbucks. I push the doors open to the store on 39th & Park and it's empty. I've missed the morning frenzy and it's all about me and my barista. Johnnie greets me with two snaps and a "Uunh-huh, I see you." He is soo cute and soo GAY. If he were straight we would be dating. God bless him and all the gay boys around the world. God Damn Them for not being straight. LOL.

24

1:00pm
Grabbing lunch for Joan and me.

1:45pm
I'm stuffed. Googled mexican cobb salad. My dumb ass thought I was doing both Joan and me a favor by suggesting salads but not soo much. The salads we ate were 780 calories. Today I'm a LOSER.

Friday, February 3rd
7:45am
It's a lil' *chilly con carney* when I step outside. I need to have on a tad bit more than the leather blazer and scarf that I thought would get me through today.

9:40am
Cappuccino for one. Joan is working from home.

9:47am
Exiting 'Bucks when I feel a tap on my shoulder. I turn around assuming that maybe I dropped my card but I'm wrong.

I'm greeted with, "Excuse me, I'm Noah, and your name?"
I reply Alexa.
"Alexa, I was watching you. There's something about you that intrigues me."
"Really? I guess that's cool."
"So I know this is a little forward, but can I take you out on a date."
"Sure. Why not?" I say.
"Ok, so may I have your number?"
Again I reply, "Sure. Why not?"
We exchange numbers. While he types I know that he isn't my type. I don't really find him handsome, his dreads damn near hang to his ass and I can only assume he likes Reggae music. That being said I don't really care for Reggae music because I can't "whine-wit-it-whine-wit-it." Coupled with the fact that I wear hair extensions and I'm a little jealous of any guy whose

real hair is actually longer than mine… But I need a new BOY so what*evvva*.

Sunday, February 5th
6:00pm
There's a buzz at the door. Noah is here to pick me up. It was his suggestion to come up to my apartment to meet and then we would jump in a car and head downtown together. Tonight his dreads are tied up in a big bun on the top of his head. He's wearing camouflage cargo pants, white tee shirt, and a black military style blazer and black boots. I'm wearing all black with tons of gold accessories, leopard kitten heels and the prettiest pink lipstick. We look like we are going to different parties, but hell! They say opposites attract.

9:00pm
Having a good time. At a lounge in Harlem.

10:30
Noah dropped me off. He wants to go out tomorrow. Maybe he is my new BOY.

Monday, February 6th
10:13pm
Not really having a good time. Tonight Noah is single handedly *messing it up* for all guys with dreads. He's on one. Going on and on about all of the qualities and attributes that *his* woman should possess. As he puts, he is a catch — an educated Black Man with no kids. He's ranting about how his mother is the perfect woman and that up until now he hasn't met any girls that even come close to filling her shoes. He then stared straight into my eye and said that he liked a girl with a more *natural* look. He stated that I was too made up. As the words came out of his mouth, all I could think was, *You Fucking Jerk!* The *nerve*. I couldn't actually believe that he had the mitigated gall to say something so instinctively vile. This guy had clearly

been picked on in all levels of school: elementary, middle, and high. My friends and I would have ripped him a new one daily. So as he was sitting there telling me in so many words that he is genuinely not okay with my level of pretty, I am floored.

10:20pm
In the bathroom freshening up my face. I excused myself from the table and have no intention of returning.

10:30pm
Got a text from Noah:
                    WHERE R U?????

10:31pm
I didn't reply. Noah can eat a natural dick.

Tuesday, February 7th
9:30am
Dipping out. Everyone is attending the new client presentation. Going to get coffee and write in my journal.

Journal Entry #6

"No Makeup"

Noah's comment last night got me thinking...

Alas, I would love to see him in a full face of makeup. To see him with a contoured nose, flawless skin, and sun-kissed cheeks. Instead, I was forced to accept his razor bumps and crooked jaw line. I was left to pretend that the dark spots on his face added character and that his nose really wasn't that big. By the grace of God he had straight teeth, which lent to a decent smile, but he was in no position to be choosey and as much as I wanted to slap the shit out of him, I knew that he wasn't alone in his quest to find the woman who meets his exact esthetic qualifications. After all, he is a man. A man who possesses the luxury that is not within reach of any woman on the planet.

The luxury to date based off of looks.

Those lucky bastards. Free to run around and piss wherever they please, while women have to work twice as hard, be equally as smart, all while worrying about what we look like. We are endlessly counting calories and buying skin creams. Whether we are injecting our faces with Botox or spending hundreds of dollars to obtain the perfect hair color, we don't question our beauty regimens — we just do it.

Men however can be fat, unattractive, even sloppy — and they're still able to land a beautiful woman. Now the funny thing about this is they don't even realize that they're only afforded this luxury for one reason: A smart woman's concern is not whether her man looks good, it's whether he is doing good.

As golddigger-ish as it may sound, woman are often attracted to a man's many successes and learn to put his looks on the back burner. Whether these men are brilliant enough to have come across new internet money, were able to land great-great granddaddy's bank account, or are simply local boys who done good, it's their achievements that we pay attention to.

I mean seriously, what the fuck did they really think?

Wednesday, February 8th

7:00am

Today is the *Accessory Magazine* PARTY! I'm leaving the office early. It's from 5:00-8:00pm.

5:30pm

I arrived at the A.M. office building and joined four other partygoers in the elevator. We all acknowledge one another with compliments and small talk. It's a short ride to the 3rd floor. The elevator doors opens up to a cool, sleek office space. The décor is black and white. The coat check girl greets us with a smile. I let everyone go ahead as I want to scan the room. I'm looking for Kelly. I don't see her, but I do see the gift bags and that alone makes my night because my barrettes are inside. It's my turn and we do the standard swap — my coat and scarf for a plastic #4. She smiles and says don't loose this and winks. I respond, not on your life and wink back. It's this unique banter that women own that keeps me going, that keeps me motivated.

5:45pm

I see Kelly. Our eyes lock and it's crazy. We're dressed alike. White tailored shirts, black leggings and black shoes. The only caveat is I'm in pumps and she's wearing riding boots. We embrace and I can't get a word in. She immediately introduces me to everybody. Sam Smith, Fashion Editor; Gabrielle Gomez, Senior Booking Editor; Regina Jones, Senior Art Director; and Liv Polk, her assistant. SO many names, soo many faces and I must remember them all.

6:00pm

Talking to her assistant Liv and we are both on the same page. Early thirties and on the brink of losing it. She's days away from her thirty-second birthday and stressed out. She too is a NY transplant. She too thinks her life is soon to be doomed if she doesn't make some important life decision now. She too is

30

looking for that perfect guy. We exchange numbers and promise to stay in touch. She may even have an extra ticket to a show on Saturday so I will be prepared in the event she calls.

6:30pm
Next in line for the bathroom. Across the room there is a lady doing readings. She has her tarot cards spread across the table and in between shuffles, she keeps looking my way. She waves and mouths, "Come, you're next." I'm a little hesitant as the guy sitting at the table now doesn't look happy with his reading. He is squinting his eyes as if he is in disbelief.

6:45pm
I'm next. The tarot card reader motions to come. I finish my wine and head her way to find out my fate. Honestly, I was never one for this hocus pocus bull crap, but my Auntie Sophie swore by it. She was Creole from Louisiana. Growing up she made no secrets about her belief in witchcraft and voodoo. Let her tell it, a woman should know how to do many things one of the most important being: *faire de la sorcellerie*.

6:50pm
Helga, the tarot card reader, is intense. She is shuffling those cards back and forth on the table like its nobody's business. She lines the cards up into three rows, four cards in each row. She stares at them and begins to shake her head. Now I know how the guy felt. It doesn't look good. She turns over one card, grabs my hand and looks at me and says, "Dearest, you are doing everything wrong. Nothing right. This job you do now is not the job you will do forever. These men you are seeing you will not see forever." She then dropped my hand turned over another card and paused, this time grabbing my chin and staring deep into my eyes, "Your voice is your job. You must share your words with others. Get paper, you have paper already yes?" I nod. "Write. I see you've been writing, yes?

Keep writing. Tell your story. It's your calling. Nothing will come for you until you unleash what lies up in your head. Nothing will come until your thoughts are freed. Nothing." Then she pushed all the cards to the center of the table into a neat pile and simply tells me, "All done. You can go."

6:55pm
Did I just get mind fucked? I'm mean what was that? If I don't listen to her advice, what will become of me? I knew better than to participate in the hocus pocus. Now I'm left **SMH**…

7:15pm
Grabbing my coat and scarf. I find Kelly and thank her for the opportunity. On my way out, we stopped by her office and she gave me a list of all of her contacts in the industry and told me to feel free to use her name when contacting them. She loved my barrettes and is getting married this spring and wants them for her bridesmaid. I smiled and said "of course" not having the heart to tell her that per Helga, continuing to make accessories will be detrimental to my livelihood.

Thursday, February 9th
10:00am
It's the first day of FASHION WEEK!

11:45am
Liv sent a text and has an extra ticket to a show on Saturday. *WooHoo!*

Friday, February 10th
12:00pm
TODAY'S TO DO LIST:
- Get a Mani/Pedi
- Try to get an Appointment for Highlights
- Pick out Ensemble to wear to Fashion Show.

I'm excited.

Saturday, February 11th
6:00pm
Just saw my first show since the event moved to Lincoln Center. It was AWESOME.

Sunday, February 12th
5:45pm
Leaving brunch with the girls. I invited Liv to join us. Per usual, we all had a blast.

Monday, February 13th
7:00am

I'm in the shower thinking about the date that I WON'T be going on tomorrow. The only red thing I will receive this Valentine's Day is my period.

Tuesday, February 14th
12:14am
Think Céline Dion because there I was, on my third glass of red *(I guess there was one other red thing)*, singing out loud:
"ALL BY MYSE– E-ELF, DON'T WANT TO BE –
ALL BY MY SELLLLLLLLFFF…"

2:30pm
Today I'm taking a late lunch. Make that a "liquid" lunch. I don't crunch numbers so a shot of whiskey midday isn't going to mess me up. I'm heading to O'Malley's, the Irish pub around the corner from the office and this time, I'm taking my laptop. I'm digging this writing thing so I might as well lose the paper and start typing. It's working. It's an escape for me. It's my **time out**. Like in sports where time out refers to a brief pause so the athlete can rest, consult, or make substitutions and *God Damn It!* that's what I need. To consult with myself and alter my plays if need be. As this all resonates, my *phone begins to vibrate. It's a calendar message:*

33

> **GET YOUR JOURNAL- TIME TO WRITE**
> **Today at 3:00pm**

As I click OK I realize that this is my "Ah-Ha Moment"
— So let it be done:

*Every Tuesday at three o'clock I'm going to continue
what I started and what Helga suggested I do. I will
stop and write. I will take a "time out."*

Tuesday at 3

"XOXO"

Valentines – Smalentines. Two whiskeys straight have aided in my bashing of this made up Hallmark holiday. Just because I didn't receive roses and chocolate or get a shot in the butt from cupid's love arrow doesn't make me a slouch. I'm a catch and I know it. I'm an only child so I know how to have fun by myself. My study habits sucked, but I still ended up a college grad. I live for fine dining and love movie dates. I adore it when boys cook for me and I even like to bake. I've been whisked away to London for the weekend and have spent more than a few drunken nights in Brooklyn. I can cuss like a sailor and drink like one too, but at the core, the center of me lays the truth.

I'm in love with being in LOVE. So even as I try to convince myself that today doesn't mean shit, it kinda does.

Wednesday, February 15th

10:30pm

I need to let loose and *Thank God* Madelyn sent me a text. She's wrapping up a dinner date and wants me to meet her for drinks at a lounge and then head to a nightclub.

Thursday, February 16th

2:30am

How do you spell P-A-R-T-Y cause I'm drunk and having the time of my life. I really needed this Girls' Night.

4:31am

I'm home. I don't remember getting here, but I'm in my bed and I can feel my phone vibrating. I don't want to open my eyes because I'm afraid the room will be spinning but my curiosity is getting the best of me. I did exchange numbers with a cute guy tonight so maybe it's him and if not then it's sure to be Kola.

5:49am

The text was from BMM. He wanted to talk and talk we did. We were on the phone for over an hour. I'm in lala land and I'm breaking

SMART GIRL RULE #1:
LET THE GUY FALL IN LOVE WITH YOU
BEFORE YOU FALL IN LOVE WITH THE GUY

As a coping mechanism while dating Steven, I came up with mantras. Every time I was feeling weak and needed to be empowered, I would repeat them to myself. These are my Smart Girl Rules.

8:45am

I'm running down this long hallway and all I can hear is this ringing noise. It won't stop, it won't stop and I keep running. I keep running and then I see it — it's a bell. I reach out to touch it and then I wake up.
I was dreaming. It was my alarm. I'm late.

9:01am
Madelyn sent a text:
>   LEX - I HAVE YOUR LIP GLOSS, YOUR
>   CREDIT CARD AND YOUR FLATS.
>   YOU WERE WASTED.

10:35am
Luckily, the office is lightly staffed and Joan is at a client visit this morning, so I'm able to slide into my desk without causing a scene. But as I plop my handbag down, I see that my message light is blinking so I may be caught.

10:37am
Effin Tim. I swear I wish he would quit. He's the one that left the message. He is having a client mixer and needs me to print name tags for 100 people. Again this would be fine if he had asked me to do this a month ago when he planned this, but since he is a **Grade-A Douche-Bag S.O.B**, he waited until one hour prior to the start of the event.

11:45am
Get Tim fired.

Saturday, February 18th
10:00am
The gym is packed. I need to get my workout in early because we are doing brunch today instead of Sunday. Cindy picked out a new place and she's holding on to a secret and can't wait to spill the beans.

3:15pm
We are going to be Aunties! Cindy is preggers.

Sunday, February 19th
1:00am
Madelyn and I are on a roll. We're meeting her main beau Joshua Abram — #8. He plays basketball and is in town. After brunch we got manicures and grabbed

Chinese take-out for dinner and went back to her apartment to take a disco nap and get ready.

Monday, February 20th
5:00pm
I dropped off flowers and a card to Cindy. She's been trying to get pregnant for a while and I'm glad it's finally happened for her.

Tuesday, February 21st
2:55pm
I booked conference room 3B. I'm going in there to take my "time out."

Tuesday at 3

"My Friends"

Where would I be without my friends? Lonely… My life would suck without them. Who would explain to me what happened the night before? The scratches on my arms, dents in my car, and the questionable stain on my blouse. I would look in the mirror and see smile lines that mean nothing as they wouldn't be attached to any memories. My friends have my front and my back. It brings tears to my eyes when I think about their loyalty. Even when I don't listen to their advice and swear they never told me; they don't bat an eye. I am an only child so it is no secret that some of my best times have been spent alone, but the most fulfilling have been with my friends. They validate my existence and I am nothing without them. They give meaning to my walk and truth to my words. My relationship with each one of them is different yet they all get me the same. I know I'm a cornball today but who cares. I love my friends.

Thursday, February 23rd
12:05pm
I sent Kola a text telling him that I want to see him every night for next five days.

12:06pm
He replied: YESSSSSSSSSSSSSSSSSS!!!

11:44pm
Kola made love to me.

Friday, February 24th
9:13pm
I made love to Kola.

Saturday, February 25th
2:19am
Kola is on his way.

Sunday, February 26th
11:30am
We did it three times this morning. Now he's taking a shower and I'm doing my hair. I'm meeting the girls for brunch.

Monday, February 27th
12:03am
Kola is running late but I'm going to stay up and wait.

Tuesday, February 28th
2:58pm
Today I'm in Conference Room 3A and I can't wait to write.

Tuesday at 3

"Sex Marks the Spot"

On the train this morning I read an article that said women in their thirties and forties are more likely to have sex on the first date than women in their twenties. As I put the magazine down, I smiled to myself and thought, "No Shit Sherlock" because it is a monumental feeling when you realize that you've made that transition. The sexual transition from your silly twenties when you think sex is all about getting him off to your smart thirties where you realize it's about you getting off.

This transition doesn't make you a sex fiend, but it opens your eyes to a new set of questions.

Number 1: Is his dick big?

Number 2: Does he know how to make love?

Number 3: How fast can he make me cum?

You just reach a point in your life where you learn to accept that a good fuck is a good fuck and sometimes you need it. Good sex is amazing. It leaves you in a state of pure bliss. It can be soo damm good that you find yourself walking down the street and catching your smile. You want to show teeth, but you have to keep it tight and controlled because while everyone is passing you by they have no idea that your pussy is tingling. Having sex and not reaching an orgasm is only something you do in your twenties. Alas, in your thirties you may still have fucked up credit, but you don't have fucked up sex.

Wednesday, February 29th
8:30pm
BMM is back! I know I've been acting like a complete
slut with Kola, but I think that me and my new hunk of
man may actually be able to build something real. I
have a good feeling about him.

MARCH

Thursday, March 1ˢᵗ
10:30am
Surprise, surprise! BMM sent flowers to my office with a note asking me to meet him later this afternoon for coffee.

3:00pm
I'm spilling coffee as I hurry out of the elevator. I took a *"thirty-minute"* - *"fifteen-minute" break*. To pad my tardiness, I brought Joan back a latte. I work for a brokerage firm and she oversees the Equity Research Group. Luckily she knows that this job is only a means to an end for me. As I walk up to her office she yells out, "Don't even try it. What's his name?" I laugh, shut the door and start the gab fest.

Friday, March 2ⁿᵈ
12:15pm
Got a text from BMM. His meeting ended early and he wants to do lunch.

1:15pm
We ate at a cute Italian place. While we were walking back to my office he said he wants to take me out again tomorrow. I like him.

Saturday, March 3ʳᵈ
8:00pm
BMM sent a car to pick me up. When the car pulls up I see that we are going to Daniel's on the upper east side. It's one of the best restaurants in the city.

10:30pm
Dinner was perfect. What's not to love about this man? He is tall, dark, handsome, and successful.

44

11:11pm

He walks me upstairs to my apartment door, gently kisses me on my forehead, and asks if he can see me tomorrow.

Sunday, March 4th

10:05pm

This is it. If BMM doesn't invite me up to his apartment, I'm going to take him in the back of the car. We are pulling up: 140 Riverside Drive. Once inside, I'm taken aback by the view. It's magnificent. BMM tells me that he knew from the moment he saw me that he had to have me. He said that there was something about my smile and aura that pulled him in. He thinks I'm incredibly sexy and that even though we've only known each other for a short time, we have something special.

Monday, March 5th

9:45am

We didn't make love last night, but we did everything else and this morning I'm in heaven. I called in sick and since BMM owns his company he didn't have to call anybody. I'm in the kitchen about to prepare my famous breakfast potatoes when I hear a woman's voice.

"What in hell is this? Have you lost your *goddamn* mind?"

Ooh shit is what I think. To make matters worse, I'm in his shirt. Her voice is getting closer and closer and, before I know it, she is in the kitchen. She introduces herself using a calm condescending tone:

"I'm Kim, Darren's wife, and I need you to gather your things and take off his shirt." She then does a smirk smile and continues her rant, but adds a swaying index finger and neck roll, "And one more thing — I hope you didn't leave any of that blonde weave in my bed."

45

9:57am
In the elevator going down...
10:00am
In the elevator going back up to tell BMM that he is a lying sack of shit and to tell Kim that she's a fake Naomi Campbell wanna-be with her ratty jet black hair. We both have extensions so that bitch needs to quit.

10:03am
Never got out of the elevator. Going back down and going home.

12:01pm
Staring at my phone. I have eleven missed calls from Darren. You see from this day forward, he will never be known as BMM again as there is no longer anything sexy about him.

5:00pm
Taking a boxing class and I'm going to pretend that the punching bag is Darren.

Tuesday, March 6th
7:33am
I received a text from Darren:
ALEXA-PLEASE CALL. AT LEAST GIVE ME A CHANCE TO EXPLAIN MYSELF.

7:34am
I replied to Darren's text:
SCREW YOU.
BETTER YET — GO SCREW YOUR WIFE.

9:45am
I'm waiting for Joan. I just broke
SMART GIRL RULE #2:
NEVER CRY AT THE OFFICE

She felt soo bad for me that she went out to grab our coffee this morning. I told her everything. I even told

46

her about my writing as I was wide open and feeling
vulnerable. She's leaving early today and told me that
I'm welcome to use her office
anytime she's out.

2:59pm
I'm sitting at Joan's desk. My laptop is out and my
hands are burning to type.

Tuesday at 3

"That Girl"

Yesterday, I should have been **that girl**. You know, the girl who throws drinks and shows up uninvited. The girl who bashes windows, slashes tires, and spray paints obscenities on her ex's car. Her "TO DO" list is solely comprised of tasks that will make his life a living hell. She goes to bed plotting his demise and wakes up with a master plan. She is the kind of girl who dials her guy's number relentlessly and then, after twenty calls, leaves messages like "Since you are not answering your phone YOU MUST BE DEAD." She drives by his house to see if his car is there with her hands firmly clenching the steering wheel because if she so much as catches a glimpse of another woman in his window, she is ready to start a fight and pull hair.

That girl is a fucking trip.

She's dumb, and yesterday, I wanted to be her.

Wednesday, March 7th
9:30am
I'm in the Starbucks where Darren and I met for coffee last week. I want to blow this Starbucks up.

Friday, March 9th
12:45pm
Walked by the restaurant where Darren and I went for lunch last week. I will never eat Italian food again.

Monday, March 12th
8:17pm
On the train thinking about Darren.

Tuesday, March 13th
2:00pm
It's been almost two weeks since the Darren incident. He has been calling and texting nonstop. Today I agreed to meet him for coffee even though I HATE HIM.

2:16pm
When I sit down across from him, it takes everything for me to not slap him but I remain calm, silent and let him talk. He tells me that he's sorry. That his marriage hasn't been going well and that when he saw me in class that day I represented something different, something new and that sense of newness is what had been lacking in his marriage.

I stop him mid-sentence and ask, "Is newness even a word? And moreover, you **KNEW** you were married so why didn't you tell me?"

He then turned the tables and asked me, "Would it have made a difference?"

2:35pm
I never answered Darren. He left and I stayed. We hugged only because I knew that after seeing him, his embrace would help me write.

Tuesday at 3

"Why"

Why am I such an easy sale? Is it wrong to be full of life and to live each day believing that "almost" everybody has your best interest at heart? Am I truly that naïve? As I don't ever want to be full of bitterness and distrust. I want to be happy and open to all of the possibilities that lay ahead.

So again I ask,

Why?

Friday, March 16th
8:45pm
I'm going to take it easy this weekend. I'm feeling a little displaced and need to somehow find my Zen.

Sunday, March 18th
11:45am
I'm doing the unthinkable. I'm taking a hot yoga class and I'm going to the studio where I met Darren. I was contemplating whether I should go to a different one, but the more I think about it, the more I feel like *Hell No*. If Darren shows up, then he shows up.

3:30pm
The class was exactly what I needed and there was no Darren. Just me and My Zen. *Namaste…*

Tuesday, March 20th
12:30pm
It looks like I'm not the only girl in New York City who is dealing with an ounce of heartbreak. Nikki, one of the junior executives, was coming in the bathroom as I was coming out. We both looked a little flushed. She smiled and I smiled and at the same time said, "MEN" and started laughing. She recently broke up with her fiancé and we are now commiserating over lunch.

2:59pm
I accidently left my laptop at home so I'm sitting at my desk pretending to work on a PowerPoint as I prepare to type.

Tuesday at 3

"Why Do We Let Boys Make Us Soo Sad?"

Over lunch Nikki admitted that today was her first time leaving the house since her breakup. Meanwhile, I'm sure her ex bottled his feelings and resumed his life as if nothing had happened. I often wonder...

Are boys ever at home crying over us?

Do they ever spend the entire day in bed devastated? Do they ever feel completely heartbroken and slighted? Or take a pint of ice-cream to the face or a bottle of wine to the head?

I seriously doubt it.

Yet, women devote an entire week or month — hell, sometimes even a year — to being depressed and working to pull ourselves back together.

So again I ask,

Why?

Wednesday, March 21ˢᵗ
2:00pm
So for the past two weeks I've been asking WHY? And today I still have the same question accept it's rooted in a different place: *Why haven't I lied and said that Tim inappropriately touched me so I can get him fired.* Today he is acting like a coked up jerk.

Friday, March 23ʳᵈ
4:00pm
I'm going to the gym but not to work out. I'm doing a fake spa day. I'm going to pretend that I'm at Elizabeth Arden. First the steam room, then I will apply a mask and hit the Jacuzzi, and lastly the sauna.

Monday, March 26ᵗʰ
5:35pm
Madelyn called in for a favor. She needs me to be her buffer and tonight's assignment is easy. I'm meeting her at a sports bar with one of her many suitors.

8:05pm
The place is packed and the guy-to-girl ratio is 10 to 1, except that none of them can be bothered. They are all fixated on the game. Her guy, Eric, is going insane. As he hands me a cocktail he screams out, "NOOOOOOOO!!" The game is close and apparently he will die if his team loses.

11:25pm
Let the good times begin. We are celebrating. Eric's team won and he is now gushing over Madelyn and has declared that the bar is mine and I'm free to order whatever I want. He is on cloud nine.

Tuesday, March 27ᵗʰ
2:53pm
Joan is out so I will keep pretending, just like I did last Friday at the gym, and grab my laptop, shut the door, and act as if her office is mine.

Tuesday at 3

"March Madness"

If men knew as much about women as they do about sports then the manufacturers of vibrators would go out of business, chocolate factories would shut down, and the scale would be an obsolete device. Men speak about sports with a passion that rivals a politician's demeanor on the debate stand. I mean, men and their love of sports is some serious girly shit. They obsess over their favorite team; they buy special outfits in the team's colors; and they are relentless in their devotion. They will paint their faces and put any and every obligation on hold for a game. Whether in public or in the privacy of their own homes, they are passionate and aren't afraid to show it. But when it comes to the subject of women, they are absolutely clueless. They really don't get how easy to understand we truly are. We're talking 2nd grade Math here. No algebraic theories or Einstein analogies needed: Make us smile, make us happy, and make us laugh — and we'll be your biggest fan.

We are not complicated. God Damn It – Treat us like your favorite team. Praise our strengths and offer solutions for our weaknesses. Stand by us through ups and downs and parade us around with pride. I mean if we so much as like a guy a little, then we probably already secretly love him a lot.

I maintain that a girl just wants a boy to get her like he gets his favorite team and whose only goal is to make sure that she wins.

Thursday, March 29th

6:00pm

Two days ago, I was ranting about how I wanted a man who knows me like he knows his favorite team and maybe that guy is coming in the form of Michael, aka Throw Back Mike. We nicknamed him that because he always talked about his glory days on Wall Street. Now, I must acknowledge that he has me a little *thrown* today. He *eventually* called "as promised" (only two and a half months later), but his invitation was soo, soo sweet. He invited me to attend the opera on Saturday afternoon at Lincoln Center, *L'Elisir d'Amore*. I had mentioned to him sometime last year that I was dying to go. I can't believe he remembered and was actually thoughtful enough to get us tickets.

Saturday, March 31st

11:45am

On my way to meet Michael. The opera starts at one o'clock and he wants to get there early.

4:05pm

The opera was magnificent and Michael was such a gentlemen. There were no signs of the prick that I'm used to seeing. He even held my hand when we crossed the street.

10:00pm

Michael and I grabbed dinner and then stopped for drinks at a lounge. He rode in the taxi uptown with me and I think it was because he was being a cool dude. He made no mention of coming up. Instead, he escorted me to the door of the building, kissed me on the cheek and suggested that we hang out again. As I closed the door, I felt compelled to scream out to him. I was having a movie moment. You know when the girl realizes that the man of her dreams is standing right in her face and she must run to him now. Well that was me and I opened the door and yelled out to him, "Michael, come back I have a quick question to ask you" and just as I went to step forward, I tripped over the door mat and busted my ass.

Me now, on the cement, laughing. Michael laughing. The taxi driver laughing. I see Michael look over to the taxi driver and give him a sign to wait. And in a flash, Michael's hand is there to help me up.

"Whoa… Alexa what gives? We didn't even drink that much."

I chuckle, "I know…"

As he is helping me up, he asks, "What is your quick question?"

I take a deep breath, "Michael, I want you to be my boy-friend."

"What?" The look of confusion on his face is priceless.

"Not boyfriend like boyfriend-and-girlfriend, but a boy who is just my friend. I want a guy I can bounce things off of who can be there to give me a man's point of view *if* I want it."

He smiles, "Only if Alexa?"

Men can be so arrogant. "Yes, only if… Michael, I don't expect you to take the place of my girlfriends, but… I don't know, today you've been soo different from the times we've been out before. I really enjoy this new Michael and I wanted to have *him* around. No romantic strings attached."

"No strings?"

"Yes, something new for me and I need it."

He smiles, like a lightbulb has gone off. "Alexa, I recognize I used to act like a full jerk, but a lot has happened. My career took an unexpected turn, and it just made me realize I had to grow up. So that's what I'm doing. Growing the hell up."

Michael grabs my hand, "The grown Michael would be honored to be your 'not boyfriend' boy-friend."

"Watch your step," Michael chuckles as I turn toward the door, "and text me when you get to your apartment."

Close scene.

APRIL

Sunday, April 1ˢᵗ
4:05pm
I'm at home chillin and thinking about how glad I am to have a new boy-friend.

Monday, April 2ⁿᵈ
9:30pm
Tonight is the championship game. The bar is packed. Again, more guys than girls. Eric told Madelyn that she had to bring me because I was his good luck charm.

11:30pm
I happen to be wearing green tonight so maybe I had the luck of the Irish on my side. Eric's team won which translates to Madelyn won. As it turns out, he put down a hefty wager on the game. Tonight he *is* going nuts and tomorrow Madelyn *is* going shopping. Got to luv it.

Tuesday, April 3ʳᵈ
2:04pm
Busy day. Clients are in town and I had to oversee today's lunch meeting. All the conference rooms are booked so I'm going to write at my desk.

Tuesday at 3

"The Ring"

Not all married men wear their rings.

Exhibit 1: BMM.

Exhibit 2: The sports bar.

Last night while watching the Final Four, I noticed that only 1 of the 5 broadcasters on TV were wearing a wedding band and I can bet that at least 3 out of the 5 were probably married. Then I glanced around the bar and began to think about who in there was actually married, but not wearing his ring. Because for women, it's all about the ring. My God, it's the one accessory we have researched, tried on, and actually priced that we have no intention of ever purchasing for ourselves. We drop hints, cut out pictures, and secretly obsess. Once you find "the ring", no matter the size, the cost, or the cut – YOU WANT IT. And when a girl finally gets her ring – then you can forget it.

A newly married woman doesn't realize that everything for her is instantly left hand-related. She talks with her left hand, points with her left hand and I swear if she had to flip someone the bird, she would probably purposely do it with her left hand.

However, men could care less. Ring or No Ring? I actually believe that they would take a stronger stance on boxers versus briefs.

Now I'm not throwing every married man who doesn't wear his ring under the bus; commitment to marriage is not defined by a piece of jewelry. I'm just saying that the "wearing of the ring" is not the same for us as it is for them.

Wednesday, April 4ᵗʰ
7:30am
I'm sitting at my desk staring off into space. I'm thinking about nobody because I have nobody.

9:45am
Joan asked me to come in early today to help her set up for her quarterly meeting with the big brass. Really the prep for the meeting was complete yesterday, but I think she likes to have me at her disposal in case a crisis comes up – like someone not knowing the code to the bathroom or where the nearest Starbucks is. But for me, having her back, is one of the easiest things on my plate.

1:30pm
Heading to the gym for a lunchtime run.

3:00pm
I sent Michael a text message:
        HEY BOY-FRIEND. IT'S UR GIRL-FRIEND!

3:15pm
His reply:
        HEY GIRL-FRIEND. ☺ ME & U SOON. SWAMPED WITH
        WORKED.

3:16pm
My reply: OK!

3:55pm
His reply: LEX – REMEMBER IM HERE IF U NEED ME

3:56pm
My reply: THANK U

Friday, April 6ᵗʰ
8:15pm
On the way to the gym I met a MAN on the street. Nice overcoat, stellar glasses, and a crooked smile. He's

nothing to fall in love with, but just maybe — he's somebody.

8:45pm
Mr. Somebody (his new nickname) sent me a text. He wants to go out tomorrow.

Sunday, April 8th
1:45am
Me and Mr. Somebody had a great time. His real name is Ken, but his nickname is soo much better. He was fun and he was actually SOMEBODY. All night it was handshakes and high fives from everyone we encountered. Sometimes, it's just that easy. And tonight was easy. He said we would hang out again.

Monday, April 9th
11:59pm
In a taxi on the way home. I'm drunk and again have nobody. Mr. SOMEBODY never called so I ended up meeting Madelyn for drinks.

Tuesday, April 10th
6:15am
I'm up early and for no good *God Damn* reason.

11:45am
This day is dragging.

2:49pm
The highlight of my day is approaching.

Tuesday at 3

"Am I Really Her?"

Okay, here's the deal. I'm looking at a Tiffany's advertisement for a gold cuff and the first thought that comes to my mind is not "how much does it cost?" but rather "who can I get to buy this for me???"

You see, after hearing Ava vent about her loser ex-husband, who she has to pay alimony to, and Madelyn's countless run ins in with cheap millionaires who pretend that the bulk of their money is currently "tied up", I'm left in a bit of a funk as far as true romance goes. Truthfully, right now I'm really beginning to question the concept of true commitment.

I am mentally exhausted by the thought of finding Mr. Right, combining our assets and building a love nest. I have a great example with Cindy and her husband John, but I'm feeling like it's all baloney. I mean is it wrong to want a guy who already has his nest and is looking for a little birdie to hatch his eggs. And after my precious little chickies arrive, be able to look down at the ring finger of my right hand and see a sparkly "push present." I mean, at this point in my life, isn't it okay to expect everything from a guy? I am not in high school so friendship rings and going steady don't mean shit to me.

I feel like I'm just a few bad dates away and one more huge heartbreak from being able to answer my question of "Am I Really Her?" with YES.

Thursday, April 12th
5:00pm
I'm meeting Kelly this evening. She is getting married next month and wants me to make a flower barrette for her hair and gifts for her bridesmaids.

7:23pm
Ok. This is getting weird. I'm starting to think that Helga is somewhere doing voodoo magic and the doll she is poking pins in looks like me. When I walk into the bar, again Kelly and I are dressed alike and this time even more frightening than the last. I'm wearing jeans, white tank-top and leather jacket and riding boots. She's wearing the exact same thing except she has a leopard scarf and blue pumps. Her sandy brown hair is up in a messy bun and so is mine. She sees me and I stop, putting my hand on my hips and she looks me up and down and starts to crack up.

8:23pm
I'm JEALOUS. YES! Straight up jealous. We are drinking and talking and Kelly is telling me about her love story, which is made for TV. She met her future husband in the frozen food section of the grocery store. After being single for over a year, she had given up on love and was resigned to the idea of just having her great career, awesome friends, and fabulous clothes and accessories. She had dated everybody under the sun and felt like if she was going to find true love then it was going to fall in her lap, and fall it did. It was a puddle in the aisle that led to their meeting. Peter, her fiancé, didn't see it and took a spill with his groceries flying up in the air and him ending up face down on the ground. She said she rushed to him to see if he was okay and when he looked up, it was love at first site.

9:45pm
We are getting ready to leave and I embrace her as if she is my long lost love.

She is like, "Alexa, what's up with the bear hug?"

I reply, "Kells, thank you."
"For what?"

"For being you. A cool ass girl. You gave me hope tonight on all levels. My career and my love life."

Giving me that disbelieving fisheye, she's like, "Really, Ms. Ross? You seem like you have all your shit together. If only all women had your confidence."

10:40pm
Almost home and smiling from ear to ear as there is no doubt that I'm a girl's girl.

Saturday, April 14th
2:24pm
Going shopping in Soho with Ava. She wants to treat herself to something pretty. She's pissed at the fact that she just wrote her bi-monthly alimony check to **LEH** *(loser ex-husband)*. (Note: **LEH** is just one of the many nicknames that we have for her shiftless, lazy ex.) She landed a huge client for the firm and has major meetings next week and wants to look both hot and smart.

Sunday, April 15th
11:00pm
HBO premiered a new show tonight. It's called **GIRLS** and it's good. The cast is all white and in their twenties and I'm black and in my early thirties, but as I watched I realized that girls, women, we are all dealing with the same issues. No matter what race, age, or size: We are all struggling and fighting to find our womanhood.

Monday, April 16th
1:30pm
POWER LUNCH! Joan gave me a gift certificate for a mani/pedi. It was her way of thanking me for being there when the big shots were in town. I came in really early and stayed at the office really late. I appreciate it, but she knows that she doesn't have to reward me for being down with her.

Tuesday, April 17th
8:09am
There is no breathing room on the train this morning. I'm face to face with an Asian chick with an amazing cat eye and my bag is pressing into the side of Black chick with killer blonde curls. We are all silently acknowledging each other's lack of space. When the subway doors open a man steps in pushing all of us into the pole. None of us say anything to him; instead we all begin to ask each other if we are okay. Ms. Cat Eyes had coffee, which spilled. Ms. Goldilocks' bags fell and my phone dropped. In this moment, I am beginning to feel myself transforming into a feminist. This MAN stepped into the subway car like he owned it, making his brutish presence known with no apologies. Yet, the three of us ignored him and concentrated on one another. GIRLS! We are soo much smarter and I'm learning that more and more.

2:56pm
I dipped out. I'm in Grand Central sitting at one of the café tables with my laptop.

Tuesday at 3

"Girl Power"

Being a girl is stellar. We absolutely fucking rock. We come in all shapes, sizes and colors and somehow manage to own every bit of our unique existence. Whether it's fashion or football, we know our shit — and each other. We can meet one another for the first time at a bar and magically engage in a conversation as if we've known each other for years. We bond between the sale racks and commiserate in the bathroom of a restaurant. We swap beauty secrets in the drugstore and spill sordid secrets with strangers. We get each other. But most of all, I'm noticing our strong perseverance. Whether we want a family, a career, or both — we go for it.

It also seems that the older we become, the wiser we become, finally learning to stop questioning our inner voice.

Of course we have days of regret and sorrow, but somehow we get through. If we want a house or a new car, we buy it. If we want to take a great vacation, we take one; and if we want to have a baby, we have one, giving it all the love that it deserves — alone or otherwise. We don't let the lack of something or someone stop us. We go for it. We are truly a force to be reckoned with. Our loyalty is without boundaries and our strength is without measure.

I must keep reminding myself. GIRL POWER!

Thursday, April 19th
3:45am
I can't sleep. I'm lying next to Kola. He is snoring
loud as hell. I nudge him in an attempt to get him to
stop. He doesn't move. I want him out, and just as I'm
ready to wake him, I pull the covers back and stare at
the opulent piece of equipment in-between his legs and
decide to let him sleep.

Sunday, April 22nd
11:45pm
It's been a not-so-quiet weekend. Again, my neighbors
are blaring salsa music. Spring is definitely in the
air in the Heights.

Monday, April 23rd
8:45am
I've arrived at the office. Will check voicemail and
email.

9:30am
Cappuccino time.

12:30pm
Going to Spin class.

3:30am
Afternoon coffee break. Joan's buyin', so I'm flyin'.

6:00pm
Going to Total Body class at the gym.

8:00pm
On the train heading home.

Tuesday, April 24th
1:30pm
Like yesterday, today's routine has been sterile.

2:45pm

Finally my time to release is approaching. Tim is out today. I'm going to his office and will act as if I'm preparing some paperwork for him.

Tuesday at 3

I'm not one for poems but today I'm writing one...

"POEM"
My eyes are blurry.
They are not filled with tears but hope,
Hope of good things to come,
The hope that tomorrow will surprise me with sunshine.
My eyes are my tunnel,
They are the path to my dreams.
If I can see it that means I can touch it, feel it.
But then I blink and suddenly that sunshine, that hope,
    is lost.
I now feel hurt.
My eyes are blurry,
They see clouds.
I find myself praying for rain,
For at least if I had rain, I would feel touched.
The rain gives me comfort,
Reminding me that I am not alone,
Reminding me that passion is near and joy is present.
The rain magically helps me to see the passion in my life,
The desire to be held.

Now What I Really Mean Is:

Got a text from Mr. Somebody last nite around eleven. He wanted to meet at a lounge. I started getting dressed, but nothing fit. I looked fat in all of my outfits. It probably had something to do with the fact that when I got home I ordered a pizza from Dominos' and killed the whole pie. So my eyes were indeed blurry because I had eaten so much that I couldn't see or breath and I ended up falling asleep on the couch as I had so much gas that nobody would have had the desire to hold me anyway.

Wednesday, April 25th

6:01pm

I'm meeting Michael at his gym. He's taking a new class that's super challenging and he wants me to try it so he got me a guest pass.

8:01pm

Michael was right. The class was draining. We are both beat. Even still, he's going to change and meet up with a friend for drinks, but I'm going home. Once we are out of the gym, I realize that I left my flatiron in the locker room. I ask him to watch my bag. Granted, I'm not going anywhere, but this is NYC and I must follow

SMART GIRL RULE #3:
TRY TO ALWAYS LOOK NICE

8:10pm

When I come back Michael has a silly grin on his face and then asks, "Alexa, are you keeping secrets from your boy-friend?"

I reply, "No, Why? What are you talking about?"

He then says, "You're a writer now?"

I smile and slowly answer, "Noooo."

He's like, "Lex, I saw your notepad. I kicked your bag by accident and it fell out and when I picked it up I saw Journal Entry #1 and read it."

At this point I'm frozen because I haven't told anybody about my writing, only Joan. "So, what did you think?"

He replies, "Lex, it's good — like really good. Maybe you should think about seriously writing. Launch a blog or something. I know you have your flower business, but why not have both. God knows you are wasting your talents at that brokerage firm being a glorified 'stewardess on land.'"

I smile telling him to, "Shut Up", but am secretly feeling warm and fuzzy inside knowing that someone else thinks my writing is good. Lord knows it's helping me.

Friday, April 27th
9:00pm
PARTY!! It's my big birthday weekend. I'm turning thirty-one on Monday and the weekend is already shaping up great. Madelyn informed me that #8 (Joshua) is in town. His team didn't make the playoffs and she's agreed to be my birthday sponsor and has anointed me the official third leg on all their dates this weekend. He's such a big sweetie that she knows he won't care. He is not at all what you would imagine a high-profile athlete to be like. He's down to earth and very charming.

Saturday, April 28th
1:02pm
I just woke up. I'm lying on my back fully dressed. I'm wearing a black Marc Jacobs knit dress, my vintage Chanel necklace and Ray Bans sunglasses. I don't even remember opening the door to the apartment. I had way too much fun. I think.

10:00pm
We're doing it all over again. Though, since I don't remember, I'm not exactly sure what "it" is.

Sunday, April 29th
1:55pm
I'm giving Madelyn and #8 some alone time. She sent me a text saying that today he wants to spoil her aka GO SHOPPING. Doing only what a good friend would — I told her to go for it and I would meet up with them later.

74

Sunday, April 29th
11:59pm
Madelyn, Joshua, and I are at the nightclub BlackHouse. We have table service and the place is packed. It's loud as ever and Madelyn has me enthralled in some deep conversation about relationships. It's weird. And just as I'm ready to tell her to shut up and let's dance, five girls come up with a cake and sparklers and everyone sings happy birthday to me.

Monday, April 30th
12:01am
Best Birthday Weekend Ever.

10:45am
My phone is buzzing like crazy. I have missed calls and text messages all wishing me Happy Birthday.

1:23pm
At lunch with Michael. He was one of the text messages that I received. We are doing a quickie because he's got a two o'clock meeting. Right as our entrées arrive, he pulls out a small bag and says "For you." I'm a sucker for a present so I can't wait to see what's inside. After I pull out the tissue, there's a box. I remove the top and there's pen, a *Montblanc*. He smiles and says, "Alexa, keep writing. I think you may be on to something. I know I only read one piece, but whatever you do, don't stop. And when you get published and you get your first big check, not only can you take me out for an expensive dinner, but you can use this pen to sign the bill."

6:00pm
One cloud nine. I'm meeting Ava and Madelyn for appetizers and drinks. Cindy has bad morning sickness so she had to cancel.

10:00pm
Kola sent a text. He's meeting me downtown for more drinks and then WE are heading uptown for OUR dessert. ☺

11:59pm
Best Birthday Ever!

MAY

Tuesday, May 1st
9:30am
Joan and I went to 'Bucks this morning. She knew I would be in a little bit late today. I told her about my weekend and my gifts. Madelyn gave me a gift card to Bloomingdales and Ava got me housekeeping service for a month. (Again, she's such a POWER BITCH as I live in a one bedroom and there's not much "house" to "keep.") And lastly, I told her about my pen. Joan told me she didn't have time to grab anything as she's been busy, but that something will magically end up on my desk.

2:47pm
Joan's gone for the day so I'm using her office.

Tuesday at 3

"The Day After"

I just saw the May issue of *O, The Oprah Magazine* and the cover reads: **How to Get Better with Age.** After reading it, I'm dumbfounded because as I grow older, I literally don't know what I should be thinking and or how I should feel. Am I supposed to be scared of wrinkles or the sting of the syringe from Botox? If I decide to have a baby, should I have a natural birth or request an epidural? If I get married, should I make him sign a pre-nup to assure that I'm not stuck paying alimony in the event we divorce?

As I look around at friends and colleagues, they all seem to have it figured out. They are investing in their 401K(s), buying property and taking the next steps in relationships and careers. But I'm still a bit of a dreamer who doesn't want to wake up.

For me, age and growing older is much more than just adhering to the supposed rulebook of life — college, marriage, baby, retirement. Growing older at this point in my life serves as a badge of honor that represents my ongoing journey. It's no secret that I live for today, but I also prematurely cherish tomorrow and all that is to come.

My breath, my touch, my words and my smile. I'm realizing that that these things never grow old. Therefore, age and growing older is nothing to me because life and living is everything.

Today is Tuesday, May 1st — the day after my birthday.

The day the real party begins.

The day I start working on my first novel.

Wednesday, May 2nd
9:00pm

I am at home, sitting at my living room table working on my book. I'm jotting down ideas. I know I need a title. I know I need an outline. I know I need subject matter and I *know* by the time this is all over, I will need more than a few drinks.

Friday, May 4th
9:15am

I'm late. If Joan is there when I arrive, I don't even have a good excuse for my tardiness — other than the fact that I just didn't want to come in. She is so cool that I could actually say that to her face. Plunking my handbag down on my desk, I look to the right and am relieved to see that she isn't in her office. SCORE. I remember seeing a 9:00 o'clock call on her calendar so I'm willing to bet that once I log in, my first email will be from her stating that she is working from home.

9:17am

There is a GOD... She is indeed working from home. Let all the church folks say AMEN. I've been late soo many times and haven't given two cents about this position for soo long that I feel like it is finally catching up to me. My only purpose for showing up is the paycheck that allows me to cover the rent, shop, hang out, go to the gym and fund my accessories business. Ultimately though, it's time for me to make some grown up decisions as far as my real career goes. Working for Joan is a great job, but it's not my *career*. And making flowers, no longer makes my heart beat like it used to. I've lost that undeniable passion that I once had. But now that I've started writing, I see that it not only has the potential to be a career path for me, it's therapeutic. Writing is proving to be a very cathartic experience. I think I'm going to pursue this.

Friday, May 4th
4:00pm

Kelly emailed me with her bridal wish list. She wants me to make a total of 12 pieces: an off-white floral &

feather barrette for her to wear in her hair and eleven barrettes for her bridal party. She is going to give them as gifts. She also asked for my address. She's sending me an invitation to the wedding.

Saturday, May 5th
1:00pm
I'm leaving the Garment District. I already have tons of supplies to make the bridal party's barrettes, but I wanted to grab a few long feathers for Kelly's hairpiece. Besides, these will be the last accessories I make before I briskly foray into the literary world.

Monday, May 7th
12:30pm
Cindy is meeting me for a post birthday lunch and she's hoping that she will be able to keep it down.

2:30pm
Lunch was nice and I scored another ***Bloomies*** gift card from Cindy.

Tuesday, May 8th
11:45am
Slow morning.

2:00pm
Well today's Spin class wasn't slow. My instructor Bethany must have popped some steroids because she had us peddling like maniacs and was screaming at the top of her lungs: **FIGHT FOR IT. IT'S YOUR RIDE. PUSH. LEFT-RIGHT – LEFT-RIGHT.**

2:30pm
I'm drained both physically and mentally.

2:47pm
In conference room 3B with my laptop.

Tuesday at 3

"Nada"

Writers Block as defined by Merriam- Webster
> :a psychological inhibition preventing a writer
> from proceeding with a piece

That's what I have.

I'm now going to the WebMD site to see if there's a cure.

Thursday, May 10th

8:45pm

Kola sent a text. He wants to come over to hang out and is bringing take-out. I'm shocked again. He always throws me off when he suggests we do girlfriend/boyfriend stuff. It has always been clear that we're just lovers, but I'm beginning to think that I may need more.

10:30pm

Having dinner. He brought African food and some of the dishes are spicy as hell. My mouth is burning.

Friday, May 11th

7:14am

Kola left. We didn't have sex last night. We just talked and laughed.

Tuesday, May 15th

7:14am

Kola left. We did have sex last night and then we talked and laughed.

10:34am

When I enter the doors at 'Bucks this morning, my favorite barista Johnnie greets me with, "Hola, Mamá." Of course I smile back, but not because he's fantastically fabulous. Because I was thinking about Kola last night. He was *Chatty-Cathy* in the bedroom. He talked during the whole time we made love — non frickin stop. It was good, yes, but talk, talk, talk, talk.

2:54pm

Conference room 3B — here I come!

Tuesday at 3

"Call Me Daddy"

What is it with guys wanting you to call them Daddy in bed? I mean, yes, we do fantasize about you being our knight in shining armor, there to save us from all that is evil. But do we think of you as a father figure? Hell, no.

Exactly where do men get off with that shit? As if women really equate sex and being sexy with our fathers — please. These are two things that could not possibly be any further separated in our minds. God forbid my father knew how good I sucked dick or how I liked to be tied up. That is none of his business. So why in the hell would I have the urge to call you Daddy just as you are preparing to drop a load in my face?

How dare they bring up someone who is so sacred while we're engaged in an act that can, at times, feel so sinful. How would they feel if we got on top of them and shoved one of our tits in their mouth and said "CALL ME MOMMY." Would that keep their dicks hard? Doubtful.

It just shows how big of control freaks men really are; their egos are enormous. They go around bragging to their friends about how they had us bent over the headboard of the bed while they were fucking our brains out. Performing to a soundtrack of moans and groans, in their minds, they are starring in their own personal porno. They want to believe that you are eternally submissive to their needs and desires.

Of course, when you are engaged in sexual intercourse, you are at your most vulnerable state. They seize that very moment to take advantage. Men know that we can't reach orgasms as easily as they can and to achieve one we will do just about anything.

BASTARDS!!!!

If they only knew:

Smart Girl Rule #4
Get Your Rocks Off During Foreplay

As for the remaining 20-30 minutes — that's just for shits and giggles.

Friday, May 18th

7:30pm

I'm in early tonight. I have Kelly's invitation taped to my fridge as reminder of what I will be doing this weekend. She's getting married on

> *Saturday, the twenty-sixth day of May*
> *Two Thousand Twelve*
> *At five o'clock in the evening.*

Wedding invitations are soo fancy.

Saturday, May 19th

4:00pm

As I work on the flowers for Kelly's wedding my mind is wandering. The way she described how she and her fiancé Peter met — the whole love at first sight thing — it makes me wonder... Really, will I ever have love again?

Sunday, May 20th

3:00pm

Flowers all done! Going to the gym to sit in the hot tub.

10:37pm

In bed with my journal and fancy pen. I need to go back to my roots — where it all started. Again, I'm jotting down ideas. I'm deep in thought. Toiling with titles and a subject. I'm questioning myself — what will this book be about? What purpose will it serve? Who will be the audience?

11:15pm

Too many questions. I'm going to sleep.

Monday, May 21st

7:45am

Joan needed me to come in early. She has a full calendar for the next three days. This is a short week. The office unofficially closes at noon on Thursday. Memorial Day weekend begins Friday and she always heads to the Hamptons a day early.

9:00pm
So this is what it feels like to **really** work. When
I flick on the light in my bedroom, I leap towards
my bed. I've been working ALL DAY and I'm tired. The
saving grace — Joan fed me and sent me home in a car.

Tuesday, May 22nd
9:00am
Just got to the office and before I get comfortable I
need to handle the first order of business:
- Email Kelly and coordinate the barrette
  hand off.
- Try and get an appointment for my hair.
- Check with the nail shop re: their holiday
  hours.

12:35pm
I'm meeting Madelyn and Ava at a hip restaurant for
lunch. I have Joan and her clients "tucked in" so
they shouldn't need me. I purposely ordered more than
enough food and desserts in the hopes that by four
o'clock they will be feeling lethargic and want to go
home.

2:39pm
I'm back. I peeked in the conference room and they're
still at it. This works out great for me. I can sit at
my desk and write.

Tuesday at 3

"Only in New York"

And the truth shall set you free. There I was – in all my glory. White sleeveless peplum top, black flowy mini and killer sleek over the knee boots. I'm giving Spring Rebel AKA it's warm out, but I'm Soo HOT that I'm not fazed. I was the first to arrive. The place was packed. There's banquette seating in the front and a couple was leaving just as I walked in. We planned this last minute so this was perfect as the wait was probably an hour and none of us had that kind of time. After placing my handbag down as a space saver I scan the room and then feel a tap on my shoulder. I assume it's a man, but then I hear a woman's voice. She's close in my ear yet not really whispering. She says, "Dearest your blouse is unbuttoned." She begins to button it and without even turning around I thank her, but she quickly interrupts. As she finagles the button, she says, "I saw you when you walked in and thought to myself, **poor girl.**" I'm still facing forward and jokingly ask her, "What do you mean?" She says, "Because I thought to myself she clearly doesn't have a husband to help button her up nor does she live in a doorman building because he would have noticed this on her way out this morning." I let out the biggest laugh and turned around to find a petite brunette. She was easily in her fifties, neatly dressed

88

and oozing with confidence. I smiled and she smiled. She bent forward and whispered in my ear, "Don't worry, dear, you've got personality. You'll make out fine."

Only in New York, kids...

4:00pm
Plan foiled. I peeked in the conference room again and they aren't budging. What in the hell could be soo damn important?

5:30pm
Finally. Joan rushed past my desk and yelled out, "Done." I follow her into her office and she tells me that she's taking meetings all day tomorrow, but doesn't plan to come in the office. She instructs me to have a great weekend and to be around tomorrow if someone needs me. I know this is her way of telling me that I don't have to come in early nor do I need to stay late.

Wednesday, May 23rd
10:21am
Kelly replied to my email. Her sister is coming to my office to pick up the barrettes.

1:00pm
Barrette handoff complete. Now I'm going to the gym.

Thursday, May 24th
8:00am
Of course I'm wide-awake. I don't have to return to office until Monday, but I can't be foolish and waste these next few days lying in bed, doing nothing. So in-between my hair and nails, I will hit the gym and work on the book.

Saturday, May 26th
1:00pm
Liv sent a text. She's saving two seats for me at the wedding. I sent her a text back telling her that I wasn't bringing a date, but my handbag always needs it own chair.

5:17pm
Here Comes The Bride. We all rise as a woman begins to sing *Ava Maria* and then Kelly appears. She begins her

walk down the aisle and the tears start to stream. Her dress is an off-white Chantilly lace gown with a full A-Line skirt. As she passes, I see the barrette I made for her hair. She looks beautiful.

8:45pm
The reception is live. I would have never guessed it would be this much of a party. Kelly has switched dresses and the DJ is playing everything from Jay-Z to Maroon 5. Liv is partying her ass off and so am I. There's a slightly awkward Jewish guy that has taken quite a liking to me. His name is Efran. I think he has had one too many because he's dancing like crazy, is totally off beat, and his yamaka is falling to the back of his head. Still, I'm dancing with him and having fun.

9:30pm
I find Kelly and Peter to congratulate them. She said that she's received compliments all night on her barrette. We promise to stay in touch and then I make a beeline for the candy table.

9:44pm
Tonight is not a subway night. I'm taking a cab.

10:39pm
I'm home. I guess I didn't hear my phone buzz because when I pull it out I have three text messages from Liv. Apparently, Efran wants my number and she wants to make sure that I'm okay with that.

I text her back:
I'M OK WITH THAT...LOL

Monday, May 28th
1:15pm
Again, I'm in the bed asking myself questions: What didn't I drink yesterday?? I went out with Efran – the guy from the wedding. He took me on a Jewish bar crawl (sorta).

1st Stop: Cocktails at cute bar in the East Village
2nd Stop: Katz Deli for a Reuben sandwich
3rd Stop: More Cocktails
4th Stop: Kutsher's in Tribeca for trendy upscale Jewish cuisine

1:30pm
My stomach is churning. Time to kiss the *Porcelain GOD*.

1:35pm
I'm never having gefilte fish, chopped liver pâté, bourekas, manischewitz, and vodka in the same day — EVER again.

Tuesday, May 29th
9:00am
Joan is the best. There's a huge bouquet of yellow roses and a card on my desk. I'm such a gold-digger because I pick up the envelope and can feel that there's a gift card in it. Without even thinking of reading the card, I tear open the envelope. The gift card is to Home Depot. I'm confused. Now, I have to read the card.

> *Alexa, A woman should find solitude and solace in her home. Do yourself a favor. Work on you – all of you. Paint your walls. Change your drapes. Get new sheets. Trust me. It will help you make sense of your space and you will find that this simple makeover will help you be more selective about who you should share it with.*
>
> *You know Im rooting for you.*
> *Happy Belated Birthday!*
>
> *Joan*

10:00am
Joan is back. Before she clears the door to her office,
I catch her and give her an even bigger hug than I gave
Kelly.

2:54pm
In 3B.

Tuesday at 3

"Party of One"

Me, Myself, and I. No date to accompany me to the wedding. No husband to button my blouse. Nobody to help me write my book.

Just me a fabulous party of one.

Wednesday, May 30th
7:04pm
In Bed Bath & Beyond in Chelsea. I'm looking for stuff
for my apartment.

Thursday, May 31st
12:30pm
No gym today. Spending my lunch hour at Home Depot.

JUNE

Friday, June 1st
7:01pm
Back at Home Depot and this time with a list.

Saturday, June 2nd
11:30am
Tomorrow the Super is sending one of his helpers to assist with my mini-makeover. I need him to paint the kitchen, put up shelves in the living room, and hang mirrors and pictures throughout the apartment. I can handle the rest.

3:30pm
On the way to Chelsea. I need to do one more sweep of Home Depot and check out a few other places to grab knick-knacks. (Note: I have never been in Home Depot for three days consecutively in my life.)

9:34pm
Kola sent me a text. He wants to come over. I'm telling him "no" tonight. I'm decorating.

Sunday, June 3rd
1:17pm
Chavez is done and he did an awesome job. He painted the kitchen and it looks great. He also hung the mirrors and pictures, changed the knobs, and switched out the curtains. The apartment has been transformed from a cute college girl hangout to a contemporary abode. The electric pink has been swapped out for gunmetal gray. The posters have been replaced with artwork and candles and vases adorn every spare inch. The apartment looks really pretty.

3:15pm
I grab flowers from the florist stand on the corner
and candy from the bodega. No dates today. I'm going to
stay inside, eat junk, work on the book, and enjoy the
beautiful new and improved *Casa de Alexa*.

Tuesday, June 5th
11:30am
The office has been quiet this morning, but I'm full of
energy. Joan was soo right. I feel renewed by my home
makeover.

2:59pm
It's time to write.

Tuesday at 3

"Lucky"

We should all be so lucky. Lucky to have good people in our lives. Lucky to have the strength to tell someone to fuck off. Lucky to be able to smile. Lucky to be alive. Lucky to be able to make love.

Luck helps to secure the future. It positions us to win. It puts us in the right place at the right time. It connects us with people we should know and allows us to stay clear of those we shouldn't. Sometimes our luck crashes with our fate and that collision usually spells success.

We should all be so lucky as God knows I am.

Lucky to be working towards finally knowing myself – Lucky enough to sometimes forget.

Wednesday, June 6th
12:30pm
It's a beautiful day. I blew off my lunchtime workout in exchange for an hour of writing time. I'm sitting at one of the outside tables at the New York Public Library on 42nd Street and just had a revelation. Every time I sit down to work on the book, I'm really just writing journal entries. Short vignettes that mirror the writing I do on Tuesdays. So my book should be a book of essays. I still need a title though; "Tuesday at 3" sounds so cliché.

7:00pm
THE GYM SUCKS. Just finished working out.

7:30pm
On the way home and sending Michael a text.
        SAYIN HI! LET'S CONNECT SOON.

7:40pm
He replied:
        SAYIN HI BACK. WE WILL.
        SWAMPED WITH WORK AS USUAL. ☺

10:30pm
Going to bed.

Thursday, June 7th
12:30am
Kola called. He's coming over.

12:45am
Getting pretty. Tonight is the big reveal. This will be the first time he has been over since the makeover.

1:37am
As **luck** would have it, Kola brought over two bottles of champagne. He was out celebrating at a friend's new bar. When he walked in, his eye's damn near popped out

of his head. He's enamored by all of the beauty that surrounds him — my face and the apartment's face-lift.

4:31am
I'm going to be tired in the morning. We polished off the champagne, talked, laughed, and made love. He's passed out, but I'm still awake. I'm thinking. I'm looking at him. I might need more than just an occasional date and stiff dick from him. I might need him to be serious about me, but I wonder if he even has a serious bone in his body.

Friday, June 8th
4:45pm
Going to the gym and then the pub around the corner from my office to write. I find it hard to concentrate at home. Many of the great writers were drinkers so I guess I'm halfway there.

7:45pm
I'm getting good work done. This is amazing. There's something about me being out in the mix of others that keeps my creative juices flowing.

11:00pm
Made it home. Took a cab. I couldn't deal with the subway tonight.

11:45pm
I got a text from Kola. He wants to come over. Not happening. I'm starting to rethink Me and Kola.

Saturday, June 9th
11:00am
This weekend's TO DO LIST:
- Go out to write
- Go to the gym

10:30pm
At home watching TV. Kola called twice. Then he sent a text:

SEXI LEXI. YOU ARE MY LAMBORGHINI BECAUSE YOU RIDE SO GOOD. YOU ARE MY PORN STAR BECAUSE YOU ARE GOOD ENOUGH FOR THE MOVIES. LET'S MAKE ONE TONIGHT.

10:31pm
I'm calling Kola now.

10:45pm
I just got off the phone with Kola. I told him that I wanted more from him than sex. I wanted us to take our relationship to the next level. I was flattered by his comment. I am a passionate, erotic lover, but I wanted us to move toward something more serious. I asked if he wanted the same and he told me he needs time to think before he gives me an answer. I'm sure that in this case "I need time to think" is code for NO.

Tuesday, June 12th
10:30am
I woke up thinking about Kola.

1:59pm
Still thinking about Kola.

2:56pm
About to write about Kola.

Tuesday at 3

"No More Free BJs"

Although, I enjoy the whole concept of having a lover, I think I'm over it. I've been sleeping with guys who I'm not in a committed relationship with. Guys who aren't my boyfriends and who aren't helping me spiritually, or financially for that matter.

I had become so wrapped up in the act that I lost focus. I didn't realize that I was allowing someone into my most personal space who actually didn't deserve to be that close. My space is my domain and I have been renting it out for free. So enough is enough. Today is the official start of my

No More Free BJs Campaign.

Now, that being said, I can count the number of BJs that I have given with Jazz Hands. Madelyn on the other hand would need three sets of Jazz Hands to tally hers. She thinks giving a BJ is a lot less intimate than having sex, but truthfully, I think the exact opposite. Giving a BJ is soo personal to me. My Lips, His Dick — Together as one. That shit is personal. Therefore, I've decided that I'm not giving out another one until I meet a guy who deserves it.

This guy is going to have to be able to make me laugh. Make my heart skip beats. Be committed to my happiness and never leave me unfulfilled. Be the one guy who isn't afraid to take a chance on me. Look into my eyes and tell me he loves me without pause. He has to be the real deal. The guy I deserve to be with and who deserves to be with me.

Now, I know neither of us will be perfect, so bumps in the road will be commonplace in our relationship — but without question, there will be love.

So until then, I will just keep leading this one-woman campaign...

while silently asking God for the strength to stop being a slut...

Wednesday, June 13th

9:00am

Something's up with Joan. She came by my desk, handed me her credit card and asked me to grab coffee and a croissant for her and to get whatever I wanted.

9:42am

I'm exiting Joan's office with my eyes bucked out. She totally unloaded on me. If I hadn't known any better I would have thought her coffee was spiked, but I'm the one who bought it. She shared her dirty secrets and confessed to affairs, indiscretions, and acts of utter debauchery — committed by her and her husband. She said that her long work hours and demanding career had put a damper on her marriage and, while at times it was loveless, she never stopped loving herself. As she ushered me out, she looked at me and said, "I hope you used you gift card and spruced up your place. Like I said, that change will help you to become a better woman. But Alexa, don't ever try to be a super woman; just try to be the best woman." I still don't know where all that came from…

1:25pm

At my desk surfing the net. I came across an article on the *Atlantic Magazine* website that plays to everything Joan and I discussed this morning. It's titled, "Why Women Still Can't Have It All." As I read I'm becoming even more confused. The writer, like Joan, has a high-powered job and is questioning her decision to be a Working Mom vs. a Stay-At-Home Mom. She states that she's constantly thinking about her son's welfare and laments the fact that, many times, she's not there to share in his triumphs and ultimately blames herself for his defeats.

1:30pm

Now my head is spinning. After reading this woman's story and digesting Joan's advice from this morning, I don't know what woman I should be. She said to just be the best woman. But is that the woman who stays home? or the woman who presses forward in her career? or is that the woman who does both?

5:45pm
I still don't know what woman I want to be.

Friday, June 15th
5:00pm
On the treadmill – thinking…

Sunday, June 17th
4:30pm
On the treadmill – thinking…

Tuesday, June 19th
1:30pm
On the treadmill – thinking…

2:48pm
Joan is gone for the day. I'm going to continue *thinking* in her office.

Tuesday at 3

"What's a Girl to Do?"

For the past few weeks it's been nothing but the gym and my thoughts. My body is stealth. My mind is clear, but today I'm in fantasy land. I'm fantasizing about that fairytale moment when the prince with the lost slipper knocks on her door. When the knight in shining armor rides up on a white horse to rescue her. When Zorro in the black mask appears to protect her from danger. Plainly stated, the moment many girls my age have already experienced.

Admittedly, I sometimes feel jealousy and resentment towards them when I hear their stories. So today, as I'm left again with just my thoughts, I'm throwing a question around in my head: Where the fuck is my Prince Charming? For godsakes, my name translates to "Protector of Men." What man doesn't want a sweetheart who likes to protect her man? With or without the translation, I know that my heart is as big as the Atlantic Ocean.

I've always treasured my independence, my single-girl know-how. But it's hard not to think that maybe it was time for me to retire that mentality. Time to give up the Carrie Bradshaw lifestyle.

Note I'm not giving up my Chanel sling backs, but maybe it's time to make room in the closet for his loafers.

I think I actually may be on my way to feeling lonely, but I am soo conceited that I tell myself: It's NOT LONELINESS. I repeat — I AM NOT LONELY. It's more like I feel incomplete. Ultimately like something is missing in my life. Maybe more a question of WHAT WILL BE MISSING IN THE YEARS TO COME?

Pretty, semi-successful, and single. It looks good on paper, but without a someone special to share my life with or a fulfilling career that is rewarding, my future is looking bleak.

I get that maybe women may not be able to have it all — but I wonder will I be happy with at least having half?

Wednesday, June 20th
10:30am

It's summer in NYC. The weather is making the change from nice & warm — to nice & hot. Therefore, I am now drinking iced lattes. It's one of my summertime faves. When Johnnie hands me my coffee this morning, he winks. We have our usual banter, but today he pulled me over to the side and invited me to hang out with him and his friends this week. They are partying it up in celebration of the Gay Pride Parade on Sunday. Of course, I said YES. This will be my first time going and I'm thrilled.

Friday, June 22nd
11:55pm

WHOO-HOO! I thought GIRLS ROCKED, but I was sadly mistaken. GAY BOYS ROCK. We are in the West Village dancing our asses off.

Saturday, June 23rd
10:30pm

We finished dinner — Johnnie, his boyfriend, Paul, and two of their friends, Phillip and Rossi. They are going to keep the party moving and stay out, but I can't keep up. I'm going home. We exchange air kisses and plan to meet up tomorrow for the parade.

Sunday, June 24th
2:00pm

I'm at the parade. It's truly a magical spectacle. The air is filled with camaraderie and fabulousness. And yes, there are a few drunks and a few bad choices as far as hair and makeup goes, but I'm in the moment and all of the ecstatic energy has me feeling right at home.

Monday, June 25th
9:43am

Leaving 'Bucks. Johnnie was not there for our usual coffee meet and greet and I'm not surprised. We went hard yesterday.

Tuesday, June 26th

2:54pm

The office is packed today. *Everyone and their Momma is here.* All of the conference rooms are reserved and the spare offices are filled. I wish I could hit the pub for a quick cocktail, but that's out of the question so I'm running off to 'Bucks with my laptop.

Tuesday at 3

"My Gay Boy-Friend"

We'll never share a true kiss and probably never fall asleep in each other's arms, but we are more connected than we know. Our movements — women's rights and gay rights — are based on oppression and discrimination. Their sexuality is oppressed just as our strength is challenged. Yet, the gay men that I've encountered possess an inner strength to rival a bull. In this harshly judgmental society, they somehow step out and live their lives. They are righteously unafraid to go against the grain. And it's this burning passion to conquer and kick down barriers that, oddly enough, pairs us as the perfect couple.

Thursday, June 28ᵗʰ
3:50pm
Unlike Tuesday, the office is empty so I'm sneaking out early. I'm going to the gym even though I don't feel like working out.

4:59pm
After what can only be described as fifty-nine of the most non-exhilarating minutes of my life, I stop mid-sit-up and ask myself: Why the hell am I here? This workout is a joke. I stand up grab my water and don't even bother to towel off. I'M SO OUTTA HERE.

5:05pm
As I hit the last set of steps, I come face to face with the most handsome man that I've seen in a long time. He has deep rich chocolate skin and pectoral muscles that push through his t-shirt like a pair of 36D tits. His pearly white teeth make me want to check my own smile in the mirror. He stops me and, in an exotically British accent, tells me that he saw me working out and must know my name. I tell him mine, "Alexa," and he tells me his, "Jacobson." He then asks if I've completed my workout and I answer "Yes." Then he says, "Delightful, darling. You seem as if you are in a rush so don't let me hold you up. Carry on and have a good evening. We'll speak again."

5:15pm
Who the hell do I think I am — Mariah Carey? Why was I trying to play coy? While he is declaring that we'll speak again, I want to make my own declaration: MAKE LOVE TO ME NOW! He could have had me right there on the gym steps. He's beautiful. His skin is smooth as silk, his lips are monumental, and his accent is panty-dropping.

6:00pm
Stopping at Modell's to get a new workout top. When I run into Jacobson tomorrow, I must be on my "A" game.

Friday, June 29th

7:00am
I'm up! Bright-eyed and bushy-tailed with Jacobson on my mind.

9:00am
In Starbucks waiting for my iced latte. I tell Johnnie about my latest obsession and he is rooting for me.

3:00pm
Come on five o'clock! I can't wait to see this man again.

5:00pm
I've arrived at the gym and am approaching the treadmills, when I feel a tap on my back. I turn around — it's Jacobson. "Hello, Darling. I was hoping you would be here today. Don't you look pretty." This time he goes through the usual: Where are you from? Where do you live? Do you have a boyfriend? May I have your number?

5:45
I've been watching Jacobson for 45 minutes. The treadmills face the weight area where the guys work out. Mmm, mmm, mmm… I hope he calls.

JULY

Sunday, July 1ˢᵗ
12:56pm
Madelyn and I went out last night. We got wasted. She's sprawled out on the couch and I'm on a bed of pillows on the floor. Why? I don't know.

1:24pm
I feel sick. I've moved from my makeshift bed on the floor to my real bed and know that the only thing that will help me get through this afternoon is fast food.

2:24pm
Time for a food run. I dare not wake Madelyn, but I will bring her something back.

2:31pm
There's a line in Popeye's but luckily it's moving fast. As soon as I place my order, my phone rings. It's a 212 number. I answer. "Hi, this is Alexa."

"Good afternoon, Alexa, it's Jacobson."

"Hi, Jacobson."

"How are you, darling? How is the day treating you? Did you tend to your errands yet?"

Before I answer, I think to myself: *What the HELL is he talking about??* I tend to kiss boys I just met at the bar when I'm drunk! Meanwhile, Black-Americans haven't been forced to tend to anything since being freed from slavery.

I finally reply, "Yes, just tidying up and then heading to the gym." (There is no way I can tell him I'm hung over.)

Jacobson: "It was a pleasure meeting you. I would like to see you next week. Maybe we could meet for coffee."

Me: "Sure — coffee would be nice."

Jacobson: "Okay, darling, let me let you go. I know you are terribly busy and… ^%^^%^&7g#5 Huteb4%^… you must be… ghhksjh%)*$%… so I'll ring you and… #hfjhdjfgh… Again, pleasure meeting you."

Me: "Me too, Jacobson." (*Yes! to whatever you said because I can't understand a GODDAMN THING because of this British accent and British slang, but it doesn't matter because you are HOT!*)

Monday, July 2nd
10:00am
Got a text from Jacobson.
        GM TO YOU. WANT TO GRAB COFFEE?

I reply: 4 SURE... WHAT TIME??

Jacobson: 10:30AM

I reply: K... SEE U THEN!

Me again:
BTW... I ♥ U. I WANT YOU. I NEED YOU. I DREAM OF YOU. I WILL MAKE LOVE TO YOU IN THE COFFEE SHOP. WE WILL GO BEHIND THE COUNTER. I WILL UNDRESS AS I PREPARE YOUR TEA AND ALLOW YOU TO SUCK MY BREAST.

Note: I never sent that message but I wanted to.

10:55am
I've left Jacobson and I'm hauling ass back to the
office. I have to go to the bathroom. We met in Grand
Central for coffee. We talked about everything. I
dished and so did he. He's 34, works for a hedge fund,
grew up in England and recently broke up with his
girlfriend of two years. He lives in Battery Park and
travels a lot for business. Our conversation ended with
him asking me out on a "proper" date.

11:03am
Whew… I made it. Another second and I would have
pissed in my pants.

11:05am
I'm mortified. I'm washing my hands and when I catch
a glimpse of myself in the mirror, I look closely
and realize that I have a bat in the cave. I've been
talking to him for 20 minutes with a small booger in my
left nostril.

5:05pm
Jacobson sent a text:
>DARLING – IT WAS LOVELY SEEING YOU TODAY. I'M
>GOING TO HAMPTONS TOMORROW. WE WILL GO OUT
>THIS WEEKEND WHEN I RETURN. ENJOY THE 4TH!

5:06
My reply:
>IT WAS NICE TO SEE YOU TOO.
>HAVE FUN.

Me again:
BTW... MY BOOGER SAID NICE MEETING YOU TOO.

Note: I never sent that message but I wanted to.

Tuesday, July 3rd
2:53pm
The city is empty.

Tuesday at 3

"Tuesday at Three"

I'm day dreaming. I'm falling in love with a guy that I shouldn't even be in love with. Why? – Because we just met and I don't really know a damn thing about him, but I'm being a total girl and already obsessing. In my mind, I've gone back and forth about the colors for our wedding and commiserated with myself over the song for our first dance. I've picked out names for our two kids and decorated our first home. I'm picturing him walking through the front door and dropping his attaché case and calling out to me, "Honey, I'm home." All in my mind.

But hell, it's a Tuesday at three o'clock and I have nothing else to do but dream.

4:30pm
No gym today. I've been inspired by my new boyfriend. My beautiful Brit lover. My future husband — the father of my unborn child. I must put my thoughts down on paper. I'm going to the dive bar on the Upper Westside to write.

Wednesday, July 4th
2:30pm
At a roof top party in Brooklyn with Ava and everyone else in Manhattan who didn't go out of town for the holiday.

Saturday, July 7th
1:00pm
Jacobson called. We are meeting for dinner at eight o'clock at a restaurant in Tribeca.

2:30pm
I'm both giddy and excited. I can barely keep my hands from shaking as the manicurist polishes my nails.

5:30pm
I'm putting the finishing touches on my makeup and then it's time to *vámonos*. I can't be late.

11:30pm
On the way uptown. I had an amazing time. He ordered our entrees and choose the wine. There wasn't a dull moment. When it was over, he hailed a cab and paid the driver. We shared a soft kiss and away I went. Tonight was perfect.

Sunday, July 8th
12:00am
Girls' Night Again! Liv and I met Madelyn downtown. She was out with her latest suitor and he had two friends that were in need of company. There were no love connections between Liv and I and the two friends, but we all enjoyed. Good wine. Good food. Good friends.

1:36am
I made it home and my phone is buzzing. It's a text from Kola.

      LEXY BABY I MISS U. I WANT U.

1:02am
I typed a reply:

      MISS U 2. COME OVER.

1:29am
I'm eating a snack and going to bed. I never hit SEND even though I wanted to.

Monday, July 9th
4:49pm
Jacobson called. He invited me to hang out tonight.

7:30pm
At a bar with Jacobson and his blokes. The "football" game is on (not American – soccer) and the score is close. All of them are going crazy and I'm eating the whole scene up. They're all so cheeky. So Austin Powers. So feverishly sexual.

Tuesday, July 10th
9:30am
I am the one who is now feeling feverishly minus the sexual. I'm hung over in the worst way. During Joan's nine o'clock staff meeting I was left alone. I stood on my desk and taped paper over the light fixtures. The glare was blinding.

9:43am
Just verified her calendar. The meeting is over at eleven. I'm going to grab coffee and a croissant. Then I will stand outside and smoke a fag. James, one of Jacobson's blokes gave me one last night. Every time I travel abroad I smoke and anytime I'm hanging out with someone from Europe, I smoke. Sure I can bum a cigarette from a passer-byer on West 42nd, but it ain't

the same. It's something about cigarettes, foreigners, and accents. I get all sucked in. Any day now I might go all Madonna and switch up my accent.

11:19am
I need everyone in the office to die. I'm being bombarded with requests.

2:45pm
My Brit lover sent a text and while I typed my reply I realized that I had no nickname for him. Weird. Is this a sign?

Tuesday at 3

"Non-American Boy"

Every American girl should one-up herself and go out with a guy who is not from the States. You may not be able to grasp the concept in the beginning, but in the end, you'll understand.

If he is British: You won't understand a word he is saying. He will ramble on, using slang terms like bloody, birds, and bullocks. While devilishly pretending you know the rules to cricket and their version of "football," you will fall for his tailored suits and great shoes. His compliments will leave you blushing, batting your eyelashes as he tells you how "brilliant" you are. You'll hold your breath every time he calls you "Darling."

If he is Latin: He will yell your name with vigilance and expect you to respond as if your livelihood depended on it. He isn't a tyrant, but he moves like one, commanding respect with every step. He will grab you by your hair, whisper "mi amori" in your ear and you will melt. The way he dances tells you all you need to know about the way that he makes love.

If he is African: You will marvel at his pretentious arrogance and lust for him, as African men are some of the most passionate lovers on the planet. Although he knows that you are a smart girl, he will make all of the decisions — and you will let him. He will show you off to his friends and spoil you only because he doesn't want anybody else to have you.

If he is Russian: You don't stand a chance — and it's not just the vodka. Whether he is 5'1 or 6'1, his sheer presence reaches all the way to the ceiling. With his slightly sinister accent, crooked grin, and fierce territorial nature, he has you at hello. And has no intentions of letting any other man touch you — and dammit if that doesn't turn you on.

If he is Irish: He is a feisty son of bitch and you love his rogue ways. He is always ready for a fight. Ready to defend what's his and what he intends to be his — you. You feel safe with him. He can hold his beer in one hand and you in the other, never losing sight of either one, because you are of equal importance to him.

It's easy to fall in love with the non-American Boy because of everything about him that's not American. His accent. His exoticness. His style. His "him." He is cut from a different cloth. Born and raised on different soil. In turn, his friends will adore you because you are his American Girl!

Wednesday, July 11th
6:00pm
At the gym and no Jacobson sighting. He didn't call or text today either, but I will call him when I get home.

10:00pm
I had a quick call with Jacobson. He's coming over tomorrow.

Thursday, July 12th
2:45pm
Liar, Liar, Pants on Fire. I just left Joan's office. I told her that there was a flood in the apartment above me and the Super called and needed access to my place to check for the damage. She told me to leave so I was outta there. Now, truthfully, the only flood that was happening was a flood of my emotions because I was so excited for Jacobson to come over that I needed to get home to prepare.

3:15pm
On the subway thinking about the lie I told Joan. I hate to lie to her because I know that I could have just told her the truth. But on Monday I totally forgot to book her car service home from the airport. She waited 30 minutes before deciding to just grab a cab. To add insult to injury, she called to politely chastise me about forgetting to book her car and had to leave a message because I wasn't even at my desk. I was getting a mani/pedi. On Monday, I sucked.

4:30pm
Walking up the steps to my apartment. I stopped and grabbed flowers, crudité, and wine.

6:17pm
Shit, I can't believe that I'm actually still rushing. He will be here any minute. The house smells great and I look casually sexy. I'm wearing a white maxi

122

dress and gold leather flip flops. I'm feeling both excitement and nervousness.

6:35pm
BUZZZZZZZ. The door. He's here. He isn't even upstairs and my panties are already wet. When I open the door my eyes are paralyzed. He is pure perfection. He stands there and within seconds, I absorb his smile, his suit. He's beautiful.

8:00pm
The dishes have been cleared off the coffee table and I've managed to keep my panties on. As much as I want him, I know he wants me more. He has his back turned while talking on the phone and I'm staring at him. He turns around and wraps up his call with, "I don't agree. Those returns are absurd." Now he's loosening his tie and then begins to unbutton his shirt.

8:20pm
We are making out like teenagers. My dress might as well be off and he's fumbling with my bra so it's next. But I stop him mid kiss. Grabbing his face, I gently run my fingers over his lips and then delicately caress his chin. I smile and tell him not tonight. He smiles and says okay.

Friday, July 13th
8:45am
I'm walking into the office and I have Jacobson on my mind.

8:46am
I must have sent out some telepathic wave lengths. When I plop my bag down, I feel it vibrating. I fumble around and when I pull the phone out its Jacobson. I dart into an empty office and then swipe to connect the call as I need privacy when I'm talking my love talk. Actually, it's pronounced ***priv-ess-cee*** if I'm keeping things all Brit.

8:52am
I'm smiling from ear to ear. Jacobson called just to say hi. He said he wanted to hear my voice before he went into his meeting.

4:00pm
The phone is vibrating. It's a text from Jacobson.

DEAREST — ARE YOU GOING TO THE GYM?

My reply:
NO J — GOING TO SKIP IT TODAY AND WORK ON MY
BOOK TTYL... HAVE A GOOD WORK OUT!

Now truth is, I'm playing games. I'm going to another gym location to take a Spin class and then hooking up with Michael for a drink. I'm just trying to appear busy and unavailable. I think he can tell I'm crushing on him hard and I need to pull back.

7:15pm
I'm on time and Michael is late. This is not like him. He's usually waiting for me.

7:34pm
Still no Michael.

7:38pm
A dapper older gentleman at the end of the bar was kind enough to buy my second round and if Michael doesn't arrive soon, he will be responsible for my third and fourth.

7:45pm
Michael is finally here and I can tell that something's not right. He walks towards me, but I'm not his focus. He steps right up to the bar, pulls out a credit card; orders a double scotch on the rocks, another one for me and instructs the bartender to keep the tab open.

8:31pm
We're hugging. Michael got dumped and he's heartbroken.

8:32pm
I'm having a revelation: Boys really do cry — imagine that. And to think, all this time I thought they were ALL robots.

10:00pm
I'm tipsy and Michael is flat out drunk. He'd been dating this chick Tanya for the past nine months and believed that she was the one. Tanya however didn't reciprocate the sentiment and this morning suggested that they *"take a break."*

10:45pm
My girl-friend duties are being put to the test tonight. I'm at Michael's apartment and it looks like I will be spending the night. There is no way I can leave him.

11:00pm
I helped him take off his suit. I've set up the garbage can next to the bed and placed water and crackers on the night stand. He's all tucked in.

Saturday, July 14th
11:30am
Michael has risen from the dead and greets me with a super sloppy kiss on the cheek. "Alexa, you are such a good woman. Don't forget that and don't let any man take advantage of your kindness."

I begin to speak, but he interrupts "You are so much better than Tanya — so much better. You are going to make some guy very happy."

12:20pm
Brunch is served. We are sitting on Michael's terrace. I made pancakes, frittatas, biscuits, bacon and my

fancy breakfast potatoes. Our mimosas are topped off with fresh strawberries and we are ready to eat. We toast and our glasses "clink" and that sound, us together this morning, even us last night, me helping him through his worst hour, reminds me of how great having a real boy-friend is.

Sunday, July 15th
9:30pm
I'm hanging up with Jacobson. We've been on the phone for the last hour. He has no idea that his nightly calls tuck me in and his text messages leave me feeling as if he is checking on me all day. I THINK I LOVE HIM.

Yes, I drank the Kool-Aid.

Tuesday, July 17th
9:00am
Coffee run.

12:00pm
Lunch run. Joan's treating.

1:30pm
Boxing class.

2:57pm
Time to write.

Tuesday at 3

"Happy"

I'm happy. That's it.

Wednesday, July 18th
9:55am
I'm at the office. Just received a text from Jacobson:
HELLO DARLING — SHALL WE GRAB COFFEE?

Me: SURE. WHAT TIME?

Jacobson: DOES TEN THIRTY WORK?

Me: THAT WORKS. C U THERE.

10:25am
I see him. There he is. His gorgeous lips; muscles
tearing through his tailored blazer. It never gets
old. As we embrace he whispers in my ear, "I want
you." I gently push him away and jokingly tell him to
stand in line. We both chuckle, place our order and
grab a table. He pulls my chair out and moves in real
close and blows on my neck. He delicately touches my
shoulder and whispers in my ear, "You are so sexy," and
five minutes earlier I would have believed him but it's
100 degrees inside this Starbucks and I know that I
look less sexy and more grease monkey. I'm patting my
face down. He even offers me a napkin. Then he looks at
me and says, "Alexa, you're beautiful."

Friday, July 20th
10:39pm
Jacobson took me on a date tonight and now we are
back at my place. We had dinner in Harlem and grabbed
quessilo flan (chessecake flan), *majarete* (corn
pudding), and *tres leche* cake (three milk cake) from a
restaurant in the neighborhood for dessert.

11:58pm
I'm lying in bed watching him undress. Tonight, it's
going down.

Sunday, July 22ⁿᵈ

8:15pm

We are at the movies. I wanted to see *Ted* but he wanted
to see *The Amazing Spider Man*. He doesn't even realize
that he is all the superhero I'll ever need.

Monday, July 23ʳᵈ

12:01am

Jacobson didn't spend the night. After the movie, we
stopped and had a few drinks. When were done, to my
surprise he hailed two taxis. I thought for sure he
was going to come uptown to my place or maybe invite
me to his as I've been dying to see his condo. Clearly
he could tell by the perplexed expression on my face
that I was a little miffed, because right as he handed
me cab fare, he grabbed both my hands and said,
"Babes, I know what you are thinking. I have to get
home tonight. I need to prepare for a client meeting
I'm having in the morning. Besides, I'm cooking dinner
for you later. I want you to be at my place - eight
o'clock sharp. I will text you the address."

7:35am

Got a text from Jacobson:

> 80 RECTOR PLACE - 5V
> TELL THE DOORMAN YOU ARE A GUEST OF
> JACOBSON EDWARDS. C U LATER. BE THERE BY 8.

8:35am

Today's TO DO LIST:
- Push papers around on my desk
- Wash hair at gym
- Get mani/pedi
- Work on book (maybe)

7:35pm

I decide to catch a car downtown. I feel too pretty for
the subway. I'm wearing killer peep toes that I scored
two years ago at a designer sample sale, a white sheer

blouse and a pink pencil skirt. I wanted to get decked out. Sometimes it's fun to play dress up.

8:00pm
In the lobby of his building and it is gorgeous — totally modern.

I approach the desk and the doorman says, "You must be Alexa. Mr. Edwards is expecting you. I'm Jose, nice to meet you. Take the elevator bank to your left. And by the way, if you don't mind me saying, I like that skirt - they call it a pencil skirt, right?"

I'm like, "Yeah — how did you know?"

He says, "My girlfriend wears those. They are really nice."

On the elevator ride up I laugh to myself. I soo wanted to clue Jose in to the fact that his girlfriend and I probably had the same skirt because it was $17.95 at FOREVER 21. Cheap & Chic! A poor girls' guide to NYC.

8:05pm
Ding Dong
Jacobson opens the door and again I'm smiling from ear to ear. There he is. He has on tan linen drawstring pants and a white linen shirt and it's open, exposing his gorgeous chest.

"Darling, you look pretty but you didn't have to get fancied up. Look at me, I'm casual."

I smile as I slide past him. His eyes fixated on my bum. (Yes, I did just say "bum" because I've gone all Madonna.) His place is nice. The decor is very modern. It's done in hues of gray, pewter, stone. There is a four-chair dining room set, a sleek sofa, and a huge flat screen. He doesn't have much furniture, but the pieces he does have work.

130

9:00pm
I'm already halfway through a bottle of white and we haven't even eaten dinner yet.

I begin to pour another glass when he calls out to me: "Alexa dear, are you enjoying the wine?"

I reply "Yes, babe, it's good."

"I'm glad, it's one of my favorites — Chateau d'Yquem 'Y' 2005. I have a few more bottles in my collection."

Once he uses the word "collection", I quickly realize that I'm probably not drinking a bottle of Two-Buck Chuck from Trader Joes so maybe I should slow down.

9:45pm
We are having arctic char, asparagus, and red potatoes. Dinner is amazing. His condo is amazing. He's amazing.

10:30pm
My shoes are off, my blouse is unbuttoned and his shirt is off. We are curled up on the couch watching TV. I'm stuffed. We had fruit tart for dessert and cognac for a night cap. I'm spending the night and will go straight to the office from his place. He has to be in by 5:00am to take an international call so he told me I can just let myself out.

11:45pm
No sex tonight. Yet, tonight has been amazing.

Tuesday, July 24th
11:00am
The office is quiet.

1:30pm
Going to Spin class.

2:59pm
Time to write.

Tuesday at 3

"Word Play"

Always
Moving forward
And remaining optimistic and
Zealous as
It's been
Noted that
Good things come to those who wait...

Wednesday, July 25th
11:17am
Ava sent a text message. She wants to grab drinks tonight and told me to invite Madelyn. She suggested a dive bar in the village. She just needs to vent and this is perfect because neither of us is interested in spending $20 a cocktail.

7:00pm
Leaving the gym and wearing my gym clothes to the bar as a true *New York Girl* even manages to look stylish in her gym clothes.

10:30pm
We all needed tonight. Ava is being pressured by her boss to become involved with him and Madelyn is considering having a baby with #8 and I, of course, believe that I've met the man of my dreams. In between laughs, tears, and even a *"get the eff outta here"* to a loser who was trying to hit on all of us, we did what we do best — *Just be girls*.

Thursday, July 26th
9:30am
Tengo una resaca (translation: I have a hangover) and yes I'm speaking Spanish. I should have just gone home after I left Ava and Madelyn, but I didn't. When I got off the train I stopped at La Casa Del Mofongo in the neighborhood and let's just say I got "mo-fong-ode" up (translation: I got wasted).

10:10am
Freshman fail. In the bathroom at the office throwing up. Iced coffee was a bad idea.

12:00pm
Where is five o'clock???? Please come.

2:00pm
Turning on the theatrics. I'm either going to do a fake throw up at my desk or fake faint to the floor. Joan isn't here, but her boss George is. Really I'm over thinking this. He's a man. I can just go in there with my gym sweatshirt tied around my waist and tell him that I've had an accident and need to go home. I'm wearing white so this will be an easy sale. You know men and blood talk — they don't want to hear it.

2:15pm
SOLD... Hello Uptown 1 train.

3:25 pm
Ode to the mashed potato. I might just hold my wedding reception in a Popeye's Chicken.

Saturday, July 28th
12:05pm
I'm on the way to the gym and then going to write.

6:05pm
I spoke with Jacobson early. He's hankered down with work. He promised that we would hang out next week.

Sunday, July 29th
3:22pm
Brunch with the girls. We picked a new spot. It's super trendy and high energy. There's a DJ and even dancing. And this would be fine if we were our usual party of four, but since Cindy's baby bump has made us a party of five, we all are being protective over the guest of honor. Little he/she can't get caught up in the tom foolery that surrounds us. Thus, we have forbidden Cindy from hitting the dance floor and joining in on the ruckus, but have Ok'd her having a small sip of champagne.

Monday, July 30th
10:49pm
I'm pushing the envelope, but can't help it. I stayed out late with Madelyn and this afternoon, Michael called and invited me to a business function tonight and I couldn't say no. The non-stop martinis were calling my name. It's summer in NYC. My favorite time.

Tuesday, July 31st
2:00pm
Today's routine has been business as usual:

- ✓ Coffee Run
- ✓ Gym
- ✓ Make sure to write

2:50pm
In 3B.

Tuesday at 3

"Mind the Gap"

Last night I was on the train and a girl lost her footing on the way out of the door and everybody stood in silence as she hit the hard cement. It was clear that she was drunk and as her friend helped her up, passengers were glaring at her, silently judging and whispering advice. One guy said that she should have drunk more water while another girl remarked that only the strong survive.

As I watched everyone all but hang this girl for missing a step, it became clear that we all have busted our ass at some point in our lives making us the Girl Who Didn't Mind the Gap.

Let the truth be told — I had enjoyed a few drinks my damn self last night, so I was in no place to judge as it could have easily been me..(smile)

AUGUST

Wednesday, August 1st
8:45pm
Jacobson is on his way and I'm veering from my usual "Stepford Wife" script. My workout was brutal and I'm sore. I did take a quick shower, but the sprucing up stops there. Even with the AC blasting, the apartment is hot and the heat is draining. It's a tanktop/boy short/greasy Chinese delivery kinda night.

Thursday, August 2nd
7:00am
Jacobson is in the shower. He's traveling for the next few days and I'm popping in to give him a going away present.

Sunday, August 5th
5:00pm
Brunch again, but it's just the true Party Girls. It's me, Madelyn and Liv. We've met some insanely rich guys from Peru and the plan is to stay out all night!

Monday, August 6th
4:45am
SMART GIRL RULE #5
ALWAYS KEEP SUNGLASSES IN YOUR HANDBAG

We are wrapping up breakfast. To say we had fun would be an understatement. We had the most amusing, enjoyable, entertaining, lively night. And now, as we prepare to leave, the three of us are picture perfect. Our sins hidden behind our spectacular shades all in time to catch the first glimpse of today's rising sun.

5:19am
Both Liv and I are crashing at Madelyn's place. I can't make it uptown and Liv can't make it downtown. We've all just hit the wall.

7:00am
MY GOD... The alarm is going off. Obviously I'm calling in sick. There's no way even a pro like me can pull today off.

Tuesday, August 7th
10:00am
Joan is out until the end of the week so the atmosphere in the office will be chill for the next few days.

2:57pm
It's time!

Tuesday at 3

"Still Working"

I'm not sure what I want to say even as I prepare to write. I'm in a state of "still working." I'm continuously working on my life. I'm still trying to figure out what girl I want to be. I'm still trying to decide if I want to cut bangs. But as I mature, I realize that all of us are just works in progress.

Friday, August 10th
8:30am
Joan has a small project for me and when that's
complete I will "look busy" for the rest of the day
while really working on my book.

6:30pm
Leaving the gym and reading a text from Jacobson. He's
back. We are hanging out tomorrow.

Saturday, August 11th
10:45pm
We're home! His home. We stopped and got take-out. He's
getting us set up in the living room and I've excused
myself. I have to go to the bathroom. As the water
hits my hand I feel the sting from a paper cut I got
earlier. I'm such a baby, but it hurts. I rifle through
his medicine cabinet hoping to find Band-Aids, but
nothing. I bend down and look in the bottom cabinets
and find Band-Aids, but just as I'm ready to close the
cabinet doors I see Bumble and Bumble shampoo. This
would be fine if he at least had hair but he doesn't.
His hair is cut really close. I then push the shampoo
out of the way and behind it is a bottle of Neutrogena
self-tanner and behind that is a bottle of Nair. My
heart begins to beat uncontrollably. I then push those
items out of the way and there is a toiletry bag. I
unzip it. Inside I find tampons, Secret deodorant, a
pink razor and MAC pressed powered NW 25.

10:47pm
My heart has stopped beating. Not only is there another
girl who is clearly his GIRLFRIEND, but she looks
nothing like me. I too wear MAC powder, NW 40. It's
obvious, she's not Black.

10:55pm
When I step out of the bathroom Jacobson greets me
with, "Finally Darling, I thought you drowned in there."

I reply, "No babe, just trying to pull myself together."

"Sit down and nosh," he says.

11:16pm
My heart has started beating again and it's going a mile a minute. I barely eat. I excuse myself again.

11:17pm
I'm staring at myself in the mirror and I don't know what to think. I don't know what to do. Do I confront him with what I found or do I just let it go? After all, we never determined what we were "doing." Meaning he never said I was his girlfriend nor did we have a discussion about being exclusive. But I did think that at the minimum, we were dating. I thought we were moving forward to one day having that conversation. But sadly, I'm mistaken because this girl, had all of HER shit under HIS sink.

Sunday, August 12th
12:30am
Jacobson is rubbing my feet. I'm on my fourth shot of cognac. I want to lift my foot up and kick him in the mouth. While I was in the bathroom I pulled myself together. I knew there was no way I was going to come into the living room sobbing thus appearing both desperate and nuts. Instead, I'm going to get through this night.

1:45am
We just had sex and I didn't move. I made him do everything. He kissed my body in places where it has never been kissed before. I made him touch me and stroke me and work to bring me to the point of ecstasy. All while never closing my eyes or uttering a sound. I just stared at him until I eventually began to stare through him. This man. I have no words for this man.

2:30am
Jacobson's arm is draped over my chest. I slide out of bed managing not to wake him. I gather my clothes and get dressed in the living room. I take a look around. I think about the good times, the beautiful dinners we shared. Our phone calls, the laughs, and the steps at the gym where we first met. I take a deep breath, and take it all in. *Because it's all over. I wanted Jacobson to be my boyfriend, but I don't think that's going to be an option.*

2:35am
I tiptoe towards the front door and slowly turn the knob. I don't want to wake him. The door is open and I'm stepping out.

"Alexa, why are you leaving, babes? What's wrong?"

Busted. I tell him that I totally forgot that I promised to attend a bridal shower with Cindy and that I would stay, but I don't have a change of clothes. He begs me to stay telling me that I can leave first thing in the morning, but I convince him otherwise. He grabs his wallet from the table and gives me money to get home.

4:04pm
Jacobson sent a text:
> HI BABES. HOPE YOU ARE HAVING FUN TODAY
> MISS U.

My reply:
> HI. YES I'M HAVING FUN. ☺

Monday, August 13th
6:00pm
On the treadmill at different gym.

Tuesday, August 14th
5:00am

I can't sleep.

9:00am
Sitting at my desk staring at my computer.

1:00pm
Eating lunch at my desk.

2:59
Going to write at my desk.

Tuesday at 3

"Over It"

Today sucks. I have nothing positive in my heart. No words of wisdom or thoughts of hope. I'm mad. I'm defeated. I'm drowning. I'm dead. I'm broken. I'm angry. I'm beyond mad. I'm hurt. I'm disgusted. I'm pissed. I want to scream. I want to yell. I want to punch the wall.

Wednesday, August 15th
9:00am
Reading my love horoscope. It states the following:

> *Your love life is in for better stability this year after much humdrum of the yesteryears. Do make sure that your desires and wishes are met by your partner. Make all efforts to get you closer and more intimate with your other half. Your relationship shall have a constructive growth this year. Better communication will be the key to a lasting relationship for you.*

9:01am
It's all bullshit…

5:00pm
Jacobson has sent three text messages and called once today. I'm not responding.

6:00pm
Going to the gym. Not the one he goes to.

Friday, August 17th
9:00am
Reading my love horoscope. It states the following:

> *If you have always wanted to make your move then this is the right time to do so. Things are looking to be in your favour during Sextile of Jupiter in Gemini with Uranus in Aries, so don't be afraid to pull out all the stops to impress that special someone you have had your eye on for a while.*

9:01am
It's all bullshit…

10:19am
Just received a text from Jacobson. He's becoming frantic. It's Darren all over again. I have not returned his call or text in three days. I would pick up or return his text, but I don't know what to say. I don't know what to do. A piece of me wants to confront him and ask him who the stuff under the sink belongs to. While another piece of me wants to be sneaky and wait for an invite to his place and once there, I'll excuse myself to use the restroom and plant some "ethnic hair products" under the sink so SHE can find it. But I know that would solve nothing. I would just be inflicting my hurt on her and that's not fair. I realize that I just have to ask him who those things belong to.

11:00am
I reply to his text. We are meeting for dinner tonight at a restaurant in the West Village.

12:01pm
Even though it's been over a month, I'm sending a text to my boy-friend — Michael. I need advice ASAP.

12:05pm
He sent a reply.
LEX — SILENCE IS A GIRL'S BIGGEST CRY. STICK TO THE SCRIPT. YOU ARE SMART AND HAVE A LOT TO OFFER. NEVER FORGET THAT. WE WILL HOOK UP NEXT MONTH.

8:35pm
It appears that he has taken the liberty of ordering for us because as I approach he's sitting there with two glasses of wine. He is smiling. He stands up to greet me with a kiss. I want to turn my cheek, but I don't. I let him kiss me on the lips. Just as I sit down, our server walks up and I place an order for a double scotch on the rocks. Jacobson raises his eyebrow and says, "Babes, we haven't even had

dinner yet and it appears as if you already ordered a night cap."

I smile and reply, "I'm getting the party started early."

9:00pm
We're engaged in what he thinks is a regular conversation, but little does he know, I'm just gearing myself up to drop the bathroom bombshell. And after this last sip of my "courage juice," I let it rip.

"Jacobson. The last time I was over your place, I found 'girl' products under the sink."

He replies, "Under the *sink*? Dear, what were you doing under the sink; you go to the loo to go to the loo, not to investigate. What were you looking for?"

I reply, "A Band-Aid."

"Well did you find it?"

"Yes, along with some makeup, toiletries and tampons. Jacobson, do you have a girlfriend?"

He looks at me and touches my chin and says, "Oooh Miss Alexa, you American girls and your parochial attitudes. Those are my friend's goods. How do you Americans say it… *Don't get your knickers all in a bunch.*"

At this point I want to introduce him to a few more American sayings: "lights out," "knuckle sandwich," and "sucker punch."

I don't smile as I reply because this whole thing isn't a joking matter to me. I tell him that I want more. That although we hadn't had a conversation regarding our relationship/friendship, we spent enough time together that I thought we were dating and that maybe even we were exclusive. But he looks at me and tells me that he's in no position to be in a serious relationship again referring to American colloquialisms, stating that he still has a need to *sow his royal oats.* As he puts it, his last relationship was "dreadfully exhausting." I have no choice but to accept his feelings, yet his answer does little to suffice my curiosity surrounding the owner of the stuff under the sink.

So I ask, "Jacobson, your *friend*, does she look like me?"

He pauses and answers, "Alexa, I love women, all women. Long hair, short hair. Blue eyes, brown eyes, white skin and brown skin." And then with aggression, he states, "I love *all* women."

9:15pm
Again, I'm in the bathroom staring in the mirror. I didn't even have to pee, but I excused myself from the table and came in here anyway as somehow the bathroom always ends up being my safe haven. My place of refuge and solitude – my office. Sure I'm stretching this, but I met Kelly in the bathroom and she gave me both support and hope. After Noah dissed me, I ended up in the bathroom and found the courage to leave him in the restaurant. And although this last time, I discovered another woman's shit, it was the clue that I needed to show me that Jacobson wasn't my guy.

9:27
As I approach the table Jacobson stands and asks if everything is ok. I reply yes.

9:41pm
Tonight can't be saved. I have my food wrapped to go and I'm outta here.

9:49pm

Once outside, Jacobson does the usual — hails a cab and gives me money. Our bodies are both facing the street, but he turns and grabs my waist pulling me towards his face and starts to speak. "Alexa, I like you a lot — everything about you, but I'm not ready to as you Americans say 'cash in my chips'."

I stop him, "Enough with the 'As you Americans say.' That's BS or as you Brits say 'rubbish.'"

I thank him for dinner and get in the taxi and as the car pulls off I turn around and stare out the rear window. I'm taking one last look because I'm leaving him behind. That's how this story needs to end.

Grand Opening – Grand Closing.

Tuesday, August 21ˢᵗ

2:53pm

And there it was — the first tear. I had been holding it in for four days. My feelings are hurt and it didn't matter if the other girl was Black, White, Green or Purple. She wasn't me.

Tuesday at 3

"Delete"

I have made a conscious decision to delete every number that no longer needs to be in my phone as they belong to individuals who have NO PLACE IN MY HEART. I will not pretend that I don't miss them nor will I act as if their existence isn't valued. But I will recognize that all of them committed some act that proved they no longer deserve to be in my presence, to revel in my energy or profit from my kindness.

And because I am a realist and know that I too can be weak at times — and a little prone to drunken dialing, I'm left to do the unthinkable delete their numbers.

Okay, Here I Go:

Darren
Kola
Jacobson

All deleted...

Wednesday, August 22ⁿᵈ
7:00am
Taking a deep breath. Today is a new day.

Thursday, August 23ʳᵈ
9:31am
Taking a deep breath. I've just arrived at the office and everyone is in. UUGGH…

Friday, August 24ᵗʰ
5:05pm
Taking a deep breath. I'm on the treadmill at the gym and I spot Jacobson. I want to throw a weight at his head.

Saturday, August 25ᵗʰ
9:34pm
Taking a deep breath. I just ate a small pizza, an order of french fries, and half a pint of ice cream. I feel sick.

Sunday, August 26ᵗʰ
10:49pm
Taking a deep breath. I want to call Kola. I need to be held.

Monday, August 27ᵗʰ
11:55pm
Taking a deep breath. I'm about to cry.

Tuesday, August 28ᵗʰ
2:59pm
Taking a deep breath. It's time to write.

Tuesday at 3

"I'm Sad"

Today, I'm sad. I want to cry but have no tears, only regrets. I regret that it has taken me this long to find myself. I regret that I kept relationships that I should have ended and started down paths that I knew were doomed. I'm troubled. Troubled by my stupid decisions and lack of judgment. I am not in a happy place. I haven't been for the past few days. I called in sick this morning and haven't left the house all day. My only interaction with the outside world has been with the delivery guy and when I saw him I was willing to take a hug if he had offered one. Today, I have nothing but my thoughts and, for once, I am tired of hearing my own voice.

I need a crutch to hold me up. A pat on the back or a kiss on the cheek. I feel lifeless because I am wading through life. It is passing me by and I know it. The clock is ticking and I can hear it loud and clear.

For the girl who dreamed of seeing her name in Page Six of the New York Post I have failed. I never truly pursued my career goals and still haven't met that one guy who was supposed to change my life. Instead I'm in a constant state of "sorta." Sorta happy, sorta successful, and sorta skinny. No matter how many times I try to convince myself I'm doing okay, it doesn't change what I'm feeling in my heart. It's like when you see a picture of yourself and look at it and say, "I look fat in this picture." The truth is, you don't **look** fat, you **are** fat.

Well today the truth is, I don't look sad — I am sad.

Friday, August 31ˢᵗ
12:05pm
Ava, Madelyn, Cindy, and Liv are waiting for me
downstairs. Ava sent a text last night- it read:

ENOUGH WITH THE TEARS — IT'S TIME TO PARTY!!!
HAMPTONS HERE WE COME ☺

And God knows I need it. It's Labor Day weekend, but
this weekend, for me, will be more than just the beach,
boys, and boats. This weekend, I plan to take the first
steps towards completing the **NEW ME**.

SEPTEMBER

Saturday, September 1st
7:00am
It's early and I'm wide awake full of bubbly energy. We partied last night. We drank last night. I even kissed a boy last night and in-between rounds of shots, I told the girls about my writing. Ava can't believe that I've been hiding it and wants to read everything I've written so far. Madelyn thinks it's the best thing ever and said that she wants to play me if the book ever gets turned into a movie. Cindy just sighed while suggesting that I change my writing day and time to Saturdays at four as she feels it just makes more sense.

7:31am
It just clicked, today is day one of the **NEW ME**. It's a new month and time for change. I can't wait to see what lies ahead.

Sunday, September 2nd
9:15am
Again, I'm up and wide awake. Not as early as yesterday, but still early enough considering we got in only a few hours ago. However, I'm not going back to sleep. I'm pulling out the laptop and working on the book.

Monday, September 3rd
8:23am
I'm up AGAIN – only to use the bathroom. We got in an hour ago and we have to be at Ava's boss' house by one o'clock for his annual *White Party*. When we stumbled in, she instructed us that under no circumstances could we be late.

1:05pm
We made it!

9:11pm
Air kisses have been exchanged and a good time was had by all. The girls just pulled off. The Hamptons was fun and even though I'm back home, I don't want the party to end.

Tuesday, September 4th
9:00am
No one is in yet and this is perfect. Going to get coffee and smoke a fag. I've just returned from fake "holiday," so it's only appropriate.

11:00am
Now everyone is in, but nobody has bothered me, which spells even more perfection.

12:30pm
Going to Spin class.

2:00pm
Just had a quick meeting with Joan. She has a client visit scheduled for Friday and needs me to pull together a presentation. Now let's be real, "actually working" this week was not on my To DO LIST. In my mind, I'm still on fake "holiday," but her one request when I started working for her was to never make her look stupid. And believe it or not, it's a request that I've managed to keep. Note: I've had a few oopsy-doopsies, but who hasn't.

2:57pm
Joan left for the day. I'm in her office.

Tuesday at 3

"Rules"

So over the weekend, Cindy and her baby bump cornered me in the kitchen. She said she needed to share something. As she put it, I was going about the whole dating thing wrong. Thus, my actions were not lending to my attractiveness and I needed to institute some dating rules. Before she was married, she set up a three month rule. She didn't have sex with a guy until they had dated for at least three months and believed that this one paramount alone is what ultimately led to her being the recipient of a proposal. I shook my head and squinted my eyes appearing to listen, but I wasn't. As I couldn't give two shits about three months. If I like you, I will know within three minutes and if I want to make love to you then I will. But this whole concept of waiting three months took me way past sex and closer to the notion of who deserves to be in my personal space within the next three months. Further, leaving me to question not what I expected from a guy, but what I expected from myself within the next three months. Will I have lived up to the goals/rules I set for myself by November???

So I am going to take this whole "three-month rule" concept to the next level. Within the next three months I'm challenging myself to set guidelines, actually rules. I already have my "psuedo" list of SMART GIRL RULES so I will continue to add to this list. Except now, instead of just quoting them every now and then, I will write them down and follow them like the bible.

Wednesday, September 5th
8:00pm
Date Crashing! Madelyn sent a text instructing me to meet her at nine-thirty at a restaurant in midtown.

10:00pm
The date crashing went horribly wrong. Her date was totally pissed. He was enamored with Madelyn's beauty and clearly when I arrived all of the attention was taken from him. As the night progressed he became more vexed. Mid-date, he threw down cash for the bill and stormed out in a huff. We both smirked as he made his exit, and unbeknownst to us, a dashing man caught wind of the whole thing and approached me upon his exit.

11:30pm
Fast forward. The three of us are now seated at the bar of another restaurant and it feels as if the night is starting all over again except now Madelyn is the date crasher and our new suitor is after me. His name is Gavin. He's tattooed up to the gods. He's missing a tooth. He's from the UK and oddly gorgeous.

Thursday, September 6th
12:30am
Madelyn is doing shots with this cute Wall Street boy and I'm French kissing the "new" Brit.

12:45am
SLUT BUCKET ALERT!! I just made out with Gavin. Clearly I'm infatuated with the other side of the pond. Between the accent, smoking fags, and their overall stylish demeanor. It got hot and heavy in the bathroom. He snuck in. I was hot for him and it felt good.

8:45am
Such a NYC night. You start off with one plan and end up doing something totally different. I crashed at Gavin's hotel. It's 15 minutes away from the office. We were hammered when we left the restaurant and there

was no way I was going all the way uptown. I would have stayed at Madelyn's, but she and Wall Street Boy decided to stay out and hit up a nightclub.

9:11am
I'm at my desk seated. My commute was marvelous. It was a leisurely walk. I WISH I LIVED THIS CLOSE.

6:00pm
Gavin sent a text:
> DARLING — I WANT TO SEE YOU TONIGHT. LET'S MEET FOR DINNER AT 9:00. BTW, I'VE BEEN THINKING ABOUT YOU ALL DAY. YOU ARE BOTH LOVELY AND MYSTERIOUSLY SEXY AND I WANT TO KNOW MORE.

Friday, September 7th
1:56am
SLUT BUCKET ALERT!! The mystery is NOW over. The cats out the bag or should I say the DICK is out. Gavin and I are lying naked in bed smoking fags and eating room service.

Saturday, September 8th
7:40am
The Brit is gone. His flight leaves at ten-thirty-one and he just left for the airport. We didn't fall asleep until four in the morning yet we both awoke early — me still lusting for his touch and him with a boner. We shagged before he left.

12:09pm
I'm just finishing room service. I requested a late check out.

3:09pm
Leaving the gym. When I left the hotel I stopped by the office and grabbed workout clothes and while I made my way to the gym, I made a mental note to myself:

TODAY'S TO DO LIST
* MAKE SURE I MAKE ENOUGH MONEY TO BE ABLE TO AFFORD A NICE APT IN MIDTOWN.

11:09pm
On the way out of the gym, I met a guy and we exchanged numbers. His name is Frederic and I'm already late for our first date. He's Russian. His accent is thick and his eyebrows are even thicker. He's handsome and tonight I'm going to pretend to be Svetlana.

Sunday, September 9th
12:17am
Frederic and I are making out at the table. He's soo damn sexy. It's too bad that I can't understand a damn thing he's saying.

1:00am
Dinner is over and now we are at a bar on the Lower Eastside and we are still making out.

1:32am
In the taxi headed to Frederic's apartment and we are still making out.

10:00am
I just awoke and his cat Ginger is purring in my face. We passed out making out.

10:45am
Time to go. Frederic is still sleep and my plan is to sneak out undetected, but Ginger won't shut the eff up. She's purring loud. When we got in last night, I saw Frederic grab her a treat from the kitchen so on my way out I'm doing the same thing.

11:01am
Mission accomplished.

- Frederic is still sleep.
- I made it out.
- Ginger got her treat.

9:00pm
I just received a text:

> LEXI – I MISS U. PLEASE CALL ME.

I don't have the number saved but I KNOW the number.

It's Kola.

9:02pm
I just received another text:

> ALEXA — WHAT HAPPEN?? WHEN I WAKE UP YOU GONE? MEET ME AT RESTAURANT IN SOHO. ITS ME FREDERIC.

11:58pm
Now it's eff Me. I fell asleep. I just woke up and checked my phone and realized that I never hit send so none of my reply messages went through.

Tuesday, September 11th
12:39am
Drunk Dialing. I'm out with Madelyn. We're at a Fashion Week Party and we both are wasted. I sent two text messages — one to Kola, the other to Frederic. May the **best man win**.

2:11am
Our legs are intertwined. Our lips are touching. He's hard and I'm wet. Neither of us can help it, but mostly me.

4:45am
Our legs are intertwined. Our lips are touching. He's hard and I'm wet. Neither of us can help it, but mostly me.

5:15am
*AND the winner is... **Kola**.*

8:09am
I'm going to be late and Joan is actually pissed. I sent her a text message and her reply was snide:

TODAY I NEEDED YOU TO BE ON TIME-PERIOD

8:10am
My reply that I didn't send:
WHAT EVVA - PERIOD

8:14am
Kola has morning wood and since I'm already late, I'm going to play lumberjack.

8:43am
Today's antics just became even more sordid. On the way out the door we shared a joint.

9:25am
I'm loopy and my loopiness has been cemented by my actions. When I exited the train, I dropped my purse and the contents spilled out all over the platform. I wasn't even embarrassed. I giggled as I bent down to pick them up.

9:33am
I'm here. Joan is in her office. I yell out my usual greeting, but I'm not going in there until later. Even after my purse debacle, I'm still feeling way too good to let anybody mess it up. CHEERS TO THE MORNING WAKE AND BAKE!

10:11am
Sneaking out and getting coffee and a bagel from the
stand on the corner. I have no time for the possible
line that awaits me at 'Bucks.

11:55am
Just left Joan's office. I apologized for my tardiness
and I get it. Every now and then she has to get in my
ass and correct me and for that, I respect her. She's a
GIRL BOSS which is the best kind of boss to have.

12:15am
Going to the gym to do fake spa day. I need to sweat
out all of the toxins.

3:00pm
At my desk and it's time.

Tuesday at 3

"The Walk of Shame"

Every girl should put it on her TO DO LIST as each step sets you free. It's that piece of fabric that links all party girls worldwide. Yet, it's New York City's landscape that makes it a paramount experience. NYC is a walking city, and everybody has their own agenda, but as you take those stilted steps, you are sure to come across at least one person who gives you the side eye. And when they do, you laugh, as the SHAME only lies with those who don't get it.

10:00pm
Kola called. I'm meeting him at Flotus.

Wednesday, September 12th
8:30pm
Frederic called. I'm meeting him in Soho.

Thursday, September 13th
11:34pm
I'm meeting Kola at a lounge and I invited Liv.

Friday, September 14th
9:57pm
Tonight I'm meeting Frederic for dinner and drinks and I invited Madelyn.

Sunday, September 16th
12:01am
I'm pulling Madelyn and Liv in again. We are on the way to meet Kola at a nightclub.

Monday, September 17th
5:30pm
Why ruin a good run. Tonight I'm swinging a "double." First I'm meeting Kola at his friend's bar and then Frederic for the last Fashion Week Party of the season.

11:34pm
NEXT! On the way to meet Frederic.

Tuesday, September 18th
6:31am
I'm in the bathroom. Last night I was kissing boy(s) and this morning I'm kissing the ***Porcelain God.***

7:00am
Still in the bathroom. I'm sick.

7:30am
Left Joan a message. I'm not going in.

8:49am
This time I didn't make it to the bathroom. It's a crime scene on the bedroom floor.

10:39am
I've mustarded up enough strength to send two text messages: One to Kola requesting that he bring soup and one to Frederic requesting the same.

11:39am
It's been an hour and I haven't heard from Kola or Frederic.

11:57am
A text from Frederic:
> SOUP? WHY U NEED SOUP? U SICK? WHAT HAPPEN? U WAS FINE LAST NIGHT. WE TALK. WE KISS AND THEN YOU SAY ALL NIGHT. YOU SAY IM BLACK SVETLANA — IM BLACK SVETLANA. WHAT — NOW YOU NOT FEEL GOOD? WE HAVE FUN.

11:58am
My reply:
> NO. SVETLANA NOT FEEL GOOD. CAN YOU PLEASE BRING ME SOUP. ☹

11:59am
His reply:
> OK. I BRING LATER.

12:49pm
No ETA on my soup from Frederic and still nothing from Kola.

1:15pm
Can't wait. Barely sitting up, but have to order Chinese now.

2:15pm
In the bathroom again.
Note to self: egg drop soup is NOT the cure for a sick stomach.

2:58pm
Ugghhh… Soo much for me taking steps towards finding the NEW ME. The only steps I've taken today are from the bedroom to the bathroom.

2:59pm
As soon as I'm done writing, I'm going back to bed.

Tuesday at 3

"The Hangover"

The **NEW ME** looks just like the old me. My head is pounding and the vodka has nothing to do with it. Round and round I go, pretending to be happy, but in reality I'm not. I'm a soft shell with a hard interior that's full of calm anger. The level of betrayal that I continue to lay upon myself is sickening. This vicious circle that I spin is treacherous. It's a selfish, destructive pattern and I know it, yet it's the map I follow. I'm enamored with lust and seduction, reaching for each minute it becomes available while knowing, that in the end, I will probably be left alone. All my heartache is self-inflicted as I continue to bring people into my space who don't deserve to be there, yet I lie – to myself. I have no one else to blame for my sorrow.

My head is pounding and the vodka has nothing to do with it. It's ME minus the NEW.

3:01pm
Just received a text from Kola.
        SEXI LEXI. SORRY BABE. BUSY DAY.
        U FEEL BETTA?

3:02pm
My reply:

                    NO. WHERE'S MY SOUP?

3:03pm
        B UPTWN BY 6 OK? SORRY BUT BUSY DAY.

3:04pm
My reply: OK

5:48pm
It's twelve minutes away from six o'clock and I haven't
heard from Kola, or Frederic for that matter.

6:23pm
Ordering more take-out. Gonna keep it simple —
hamburger and french fries.

7:00pm
I feel better, but still nothing from Frederic or Kola.

7:45pm
Just received a text from Frederic.
        I COME NOW. I GOT SOUP. WHAT IS ADDRESS?

7:46pm
I didn't send a reply to Frederic. It's been damn near
eight hours since my first text requesting soup. I
can't, as the **NEW ME** wouldn't.

8:33pm
Just received a text from Kola.
        BABE – MAY NOT GET THERE TILL TEN.
        BUSY DAY. U FEEL BETTA?

8:34pm
I didn't send a reply to Kola either. I can't, as the
NEW ME wouldn't.

11:00pm
Finally leaving the house for the first time today. I
need Gatorade from the deli.

11:17pm
Frederic has left three messages and I've received six
more text messages from Kola, but I'm not returning a
single text or call as they both proved that neither is
the *best man*. **Today — NOBODY WON.**

Wednesday, September 19ᵗʰ
2:01am
The realization that I can no longer see Kola anymore
has me wide awake and I can't sleep. As I flip channels
something becomes clear — my next SMART GIRL RULE.
I grab my fancy pen and journal which is on the
nightstand and I write:

Smart Girl Rule #6

Be a Smart Girl

7:15am
The alarm just went off. I hit snooze and pull the
covers tight. I want a few more minutes to think. I
know that I must actually try to be smart. I know, that
going forward I can't do the same shit. I just can't. I
have to follow my rules.

9:59am
At the office, but I don't want to be here. The
easiness of this job is now becoming a burden. It no
longer feels like the SMART thing to do.

1:00pm
Taking a boxing class.

5:30pm
Taking a Spin class.

8:54pm
I stopped at the dive bar on the upper Westside. I thought I would be able to write, but nothing.

Thursday, September 20th
12:01am
The race is still on. I've received five calls and six text messages from Kola and only three text messages and two phone calls from Frederic.

12:02am
I'm sticking to the rules. No calls. No text messages.

3:33am
Can't sleep. Grabbing my journal and pen from the night stand. I might as well try to write.

8:33am
Damn It. I over slept. I'm going to be late.

9:44am
Just arrived and Joan's pissed again.

10:15am
At 'Bucks and Johnnie isn't even here today to make me smile.

2:33pm
Went to the gym and now back at the office. I wish I could have stayed in the steam room all day.

7:09pm
At the dive bar and it's Tequila Thursdays.

11:04pm
On the way home on the train reading what I attempted to write and none of it makes sense.

Friday, September 21st
9:15am
Joan is out today and for once this doesn't even matter as I've mentally checked out of this job.

1:00pm
Taking boxing class.

3:15pm
BEST MAN UPDATE! Frederic is in the lead with five calls and five text messages. But, Kola is holding a close second with four text messages and three calls.

6:00pm
I'm home and in for the night. I stopped and got wine and will order takeout. My plan is to get some writing done.

11:00pm
I feel alone. That's the last sentence I wrote. Actually, that's the only fluent sentence I've written all night. Tonight's writing session is a bust.

Saturday, September 22nd
4:01am
Can't sleep.

6:06pm
Home from the gym. Tonight I'm going to keep it local and try to get some writing done at a bar in the neighborhood.

11:22pm
The appetizers were great. The drinks were great. My writing was not great. I was able to come up with absolutely nothing.

Sunday, September 23rd
10:01am
I still feel alone. I need my friends. I left messages
for Madelyn, Ava, Cindy, and Liv.

4:03pm
The "best man" contest is coming to an end. Today we
have a tie – one text message from each.

8:13pm
It's confirmed! Meeting up with girls on Wednesday.
This is the highlight of the day.

Monday, September 24th
3:15pm
Same shit different day. Joan left early. Tim needed
help with his meeting and I went to the gym.

Tuesday, September 25th
11:33am
Quiet morning. Joan and her directs are at an offsite
meeting until late afternoon. I thought I would be
able to get some writing done but again, nothing is
coming out.

2:59pm
It's time.

Tuesday at 3

"Screw Me"

Nothing is working. Drinking is neither numbing my pain nor exciting my creativity.

I'm fucked...

Wednesday, September 26th
7:00pm
I'm the first to arrive. I'm meeting Ava, Madelyn, Cindy, and Liv at a tapas bar in Union Square. I'm soo excited. I need this.

11:00pm
The contest is back on! Except there's one little change.

When I got home and checked my phone, I had four text messages:

One from Cindy – she wants to do lunch ASAP.
One from Ava – she's wants me to be her +1 at an event tomorrow.
One from Madelyn – she needs me to "date crash" on Saturday.
One from Liv – she wants to set up dinner with us and Kelly.

FINAL SCORE
"BEST MAN"   **0**
"BEST GIRL(s)"   **4**

Friday, September 28th
9:15am
Coffee time.

Saturday, September 29th
1:00pm
On my way to the gym and then going shopping. The weather is changing and I want to grab some new pieces.

10:30pm
Leaving now to meet Madelyn.

Sunday, September 30th
2:30pm
Last night was fun. Madelyn's date Kelvin was soo cool. Soo cool that he invited me to join them this afternoon for brunch. Sometimes date crashing works out just fine.

OCTOBER

Monday, October 1st
8:30am
Early day. Joan's boss is in and she wanted me here.

10:01am
Coffee break. *Joan's buying and I'm flying.*

12:34pm
"POWER LUNCH"
I'm going to the gym and taking a weight lifting class.

5:30pm
Going for a quick run then going to write.

9:44pm
I'm home. I stopped at the store and grabbed food. I'm going to cook. On the train I was thinking about how I'm soo quick to cook for a guy, but never take the time to prepare dinner for myself.

Tuesday, October 2nd
9:01am
Nobody's in this morning. I checked voicemail and now it's cappuccino time.

9:15am
I'm back and not alone. A few of Joan's directs are in, but I want to quickly pick up where I left off writing yesterday and finish my thoughts. I'm running with this whole SMART GIRL RULES concept.

11:01am
Joan called and now I have stuff to do.

12:48pm
Taking a one o'clock class. Joan sent an email and will be in a little after two.

2:45pm
Staying at my desk to write and it has to be quick. Joan said she needs to see me after her conf call.

Tuesday at 3

"It's Back"

My smile is back and it's not a closed-lip grin. It's a wide, show all your teeth, commercial expression of joy. Last month kicked my ass and today I'm on my way to feeling like **finally** and I know exactly how I got here. **My Rules**.

I must follow my rules. ☺

3:43pm
OMG... I just got served. I thought I was the one who was "over it", but it's Joan who's "over me." She just delicately let me have it. She's worried about me, concerned that I'm wasting time. She just gave me an ultimatum: I either commit to my writing or commit to this job as her assistant – and that was it. I guess this was her way of telling me that I've been slacking off and she's right.

8:00pm
Leaving the gym and Jacobson was there. He stopped me. But this time as his lips moved I didn't. He no longer has me mesmerized.

Wednesday, October 3rd
11:49am
Easy morning.

6:01pm
Going to the gym and then home to cook dinner, drink wine, and work on the book.

9:02pm
Just got a text. The number isn't saved, but I know who it is:

LEXI LET'S HOOK UP THIS WEEK

10:57pm
Never returned Kola's text. Going to bed.

Thursday, October 4th
8:25am
I'm up and in a frantic tizzy. On my way out the door, I received a text from Liv. She set up dinner with Kelly tonight. We are going to a cute place in the Meat Packing District so I'm trying to figure out what I'm going to wear and time is ticking. I can't be late today.

9:29am
Made it!

1:20pm
There's a one-thirty Pilates class and I'm on the way.

5:30pm
Joan's outta here and so am I. I am going for a quick run and then shower and change. We are meeting at eight o'clock.

8:25pm
The train was crawling so I'm late. My only hope is that both Liv and Kelly were running late too.

8:37pm
I spot Liv. She's at the bar.

8:47pm
Kelly is running late. Liv was early and I arrived right on time. She has a shot waiting for me.

9:11pm
Appetizers and drinks are coming from every direction. The bartender is one of Liv's friends and the manager of the restaurant turned out to be an old colleague of Kelly's.

9:58pm
After ordering our last round, Kelly states that she has an announcement: the real reason that she had Liv set up dinner. Next month she's launching a magazine and Liv is taking a position in the p.r. department leaving her in need of a new personal assistant and the job is mine if I want it.

10:01pm
We all are cracking up. I got soo excited that when I jumped up to say "HELL YEAH", I spilled all of our

drinks. Working with Kelly and Liv will be a great opportunity for me. Excited doesn't even began to express how I feel.

11:33pm
Liv and I split a cab uptown and I'm almost home.

11:52pm
I'm in. I sent a text to Liv thanking her for tonight. I know she played a big part in suggesting that I take her old job.

Friday, October 5th
7:17am
Last night was unreal. Before I get out of the bed I'm surfing the net to see what my horoscope was yesterday.

> *The planets suggest that you are frustrated at being ignored so take solace in this quiet time and think.*

7:18am
IGNORED??? Total B.S. Where's Helga when you need her??

9:17am
Joan is out today and next week clients are in town so I have a small TO DO LIST that must be completed by the end of the day.

10:45am
Last minute coffee run for a few of the guys. I hope Johnnie is there so I can tell him my news.

10:57am
Johnnie isn't happy. My new office will be in Soho so we will only see each other if we set up play dates.

12:31pm
I'm skipping the gym today in favor of writing at the pub around the corner. I haven't been there in ages.

Sunday, October 7th

11:03pm

Kola called all day. Kola sent text messages all day. I stayed focused on me all day.

Monday, October 8th

5:01pm

Today was nonstop and thank God it's over. I'm taking a six o'clock class then heading straight home.

7:22pm

Detour. I stopped at 'Bucks. I needed to write. I saw Jacobson again. We ran into each other on the same step where we first met. He grabbed my waist, smiled, and in his deliciously sexy accent asked how I was doing. I said fine; except I was telling a lie. I'm doing better than fine because I'm done – done being stupid. No more one night stands. No more guys who leave one half of me feeling empty.

9:10pm

Taking a scone to go. I will continue my writing session when I get home.

Tuesday, October 9th

7:05am

Calling in sick. I awoke with soo many thoughts going through my head that I must stay home and write. On the surface it appears as if my time at the brokerage firm has all been in vain, but that couldn't be the farthest sentiment from the truth. I've been quietly paying attention and right now – in the corporate world, it's the fourth quarter – and every smart company uses this time to assess and prepare.☺ It's time to lay off the lowest performers and make use of unused resources. Time to realign strategy and prepare for next year's growth and that's exactly what I'm about to do – Alexa Ross Inc. is officially going through a restructure.

11:19am
Still writing. I'm on a roll.

1:01pm
Taking a break. Going out to get some air and grab take-out from the restaurant on the corner.

2:57pm
Back at the apartment in the nick of time to write. I ended up talking to a guy at the restaurant. He convinced me to stay, eat, and have a few beers. When the bill came he insisted that he pay and when it was time to leave, he didn't ask for my number or suggest we hook up again. He was sweet. His name was Juan and he left me thinking.

Tuesday at 3

"Finally"

Finally, I'm beginning to see the light at the end of the tunnel and it has me excited. I can't wait for all my dreams to come true. I can't wait to no longer have to hold back tears, as I finally will have no reason to cry.

I can't wait to stop wishing for the boy that can't live without me or wondering about the career that will fulfill me because I will have both.

I can't wait.

Wednesday, October 10th

8:31am
On the train thinking about when and how I'm going to tell Joan that I'm quitting. There is no way in Hell that I'm turning the job with Kelly down.

9:15am
At the office. Checked email and Joan will be in by ten.

10:49am
Going in Joan's office.

11:00am
Grabbing coffee. Joan couldn't be happier. She's more excited for me than I think I am for myself. She supports my move 100%. She didn't want to continue our conversation without coffee.

11:30am
Back at my desk. My smile — it just keeps getting bigger. I have Joan's blessings and Kelly's nod. I'm leaving the brokerage firm at the end of the month — what a lucky girl I am.

1:45pm
Gym time.

3:00pm
Guess who? Jacobson just called and left a voicemail.

"Dear it's me, Jacobson. I want to prepare dinner for you. I'm not traveling for the next three weeks so let me know what's best. And one more thing — the items under the sink in the loo are gone. That should make you feel good. That girl ended up being rubbish. I'll tell you more when you come over"

3:01pm
Guess what? I'm not calling him back and I'm not coming over.

5:11pm
Kelly just returned my text. I start at the magazine on November 5th. Woohoo!

9:03pm
At home and my phone is buzzing like crazy. I look down and again it's Jacobson. It's another missed call and a text message.

9:47pm
I had no intention of writing tonight, but something just popped in my head and I must put it on paper. These recent calls and text messages from both Kola and Jacobson have me feeling more like third base than home plate. It's as if they are only calling because their schedules have somehow been freed and not because they REALLY miss me leaving me to create a new rule:

SMART GIRL RULE #7
NEVER BE THE PENCIL IN BITCH

11:59pm
I ended up writing good stuff tonight and now my SMART ASS is going to bed.

Friday, October 12th
11:09am
Easy morning. Meeting Cindy at six. She's finally feeling well. She's in the last trimester and her little bundle of joy is kicking her butt. She's been rescheduling on me ever since we all met up two weeks ago.

7:35pm
Tag — I'm IT. Cindy wants me to plan her baby shower while she plans my love life. I was her unlikely second choice by default. Her sister Paige just closed on a new apartment and she has to be out of her old place by the end of month so she no longer has time to be in charge. The good news is that the bulk of the work is done. The date is set; October 28th, the venue is secured, the

RSVPs are in, and the caterer confirmed. My only true job is to show up and be the *Hostess with the Most-isss.* When the bill came, she grabbed it announcing that tonight was her treat. I laughed and said, "No shit." It's only her treat because she wanted me to be tipsy enough to say yes to her request and for not leaving her in the restaurant as she spent the entire dinner lecturing me about dating and relationships.

7:49pm
It's major traffic on the Westside Highway. We split a cab uptown and when Cindy got out, she handed me a shopping bag and told me not to open it until I got home. Of course I was not listening to her but just as I was going to defy her wishes Madelyn called and we ended up talking the whole ride home.

8:29pm
Finally home and about to open the bag.

8:35pm
BOOKS… The bag contains three books and a hand written note from Cindy

> 3 books for you to read.
>
> I've never seen you read a book so I can't understand how you could possibly attempt to write one without reading a few first.
>
> Enjoy. Cindy (my treat) ☺

9:12pm
I'm on the couch. I have a glass of wine and my homework from Cindy, my three books: *Half of a Yellow Sun*; *Think Like a Man, Act Like a Lady*; and *#GIRLBOSS*.

10:17pm
I haven't opened any of the books. I'm back on the phone with Madelyn and more than half way through the bottle of wine.

10:33pm
I just received a text.
                LEXI — WHATS UP? I MISS U.
Again, it's Kola..

10:46pm
It's time to start my homework. It's time to read. While I was on the phone with Madelyn, I missed a text message from Cindy. She sent reading instructions. She wants me to start with *Think Like a Man, Act Like a Lady*, then *Half of a Yellow Sun,* and lastly *#GIRLBOSS*.

Saturday, October 13th
5:03am
I fell asleep on the couch and didn't end up reading shit. Moving to the bed now.

11:01am
Still in bed and on page forty-four from book #1 on Cindy's list. I've never been a book reader; only a magazine/newspaper reader so this whole experience kinda has me excited.

Sunday, October 14th
2:09pm
Hitting the gym, going to write and then continue to read.

Monday, October 15th
1:00pm
Easy morning. A few of the guys needed help with travel and scheduling and when I return from the gym I have a small project to work on for Joan.

6:00pm
At the gym again — pulling a two-a-day.

6:03pm
I just spotted Jacobson and he's approaching me with a perplexed look and as he gets closer he starts to speak:

"Dear, did you get my messages? Is everything okay? I want to cook for you? He then begins to chuckle and says, "And the loo is now yours. I even bought more Band-Aids." Again he asks, "Did you get my message?"

I reply, "Yes, I got it. But as you Brits say, **PISS OFF** and as us American Girls say *I CAN'T EVEN WITH YOU*."

I pause and continue, "I think you are just looking for a good time and I've started to make some true changes in my life and now realize that I not only want a guy to have fun with, but one who both needs and appreciates me."

He then grabs my face and gives me the biggest sloppiest kiss on the cheek and says, "You are lovely Alexa, simply brilliant. I wish nothing but goodness for you and as us Brits say, *Keep Calm and Carry On.* I'll see you around."

8:09pm
Again, I'm feeling soo SMART. I'm done being stupid. I'm going to the dive bar to write for an hour and then going home to read.

Tuesday, October 16th
9:00am
At the office on count down. Today I will let Joan know that my last day is Friday, November 3rd.

11:00am
Joan is totally cool with me leaving and we are going to start interviewing for my replacement next week. Believe it or not, Tim has a niece that he thinks will

be perfect for the job. Let's just hope the "stupid gene" that he got stuck with skipped a generation.

1:31pm
No gym. Going to the pub to continue my *required reading.*

2:40pm
Back at the office. I have to book some travel then I'm going to write.

Tuesday at 3

"Think Like a Man"

Think Like a Man? Really?

I watch them — men — every day, and piece by piece I see their weaknesses:

They're driven by perceived innocence, moved by money, and naive to the obvious. So to think like THEM would be the most stupid shit on Earth.

As thinking LIKE A woman would prove to be much more efficient because we have the strength to persevere even while we hurt, have the ability to demonstrate power even as we cry, and if pushed can flawlessly manipulate through obstacles and set backs.

So on the contrary,

a Man should want to THINK LIKE US.

192

Thursday, October 18th

11:01am

This morning has been busy and this afternoon isn't going to slow down. Even though Tim is pushing his niece for the job, Joan is still interviewing. We've already seen three candidates and the next one is scheduled for eleven-thirty.

11:51am

At the gym. The last candidate, Roxanne, was hilarious. She was a pampered princess who obviously was just going on interviews to appease Daddy. When I greeted her at the door of the firm, she was on the phone. She abruptly ended her call and before even asking my name she wanted directions to the bathroom. When she returned, she complimented my hair and asked how long did I think this whole interview "thing" would take. Joan spent ten minutes with her and when she walked out of her office, she glanced at me with annoyance and told me to have a good day.

1:16pm

Back from the gym with a little time to kill before the next round of interviews. Even though I believe it's all bullshit, I'm still doing a skim read of book #1 on Cindy's list. I've come across a passage that describes when the author's girlfriend walks out on him and now realize the whole reverse psychology message that the novel is based on. It's a manual written by a man that gives instruction on how to deal with a man's shortcomings while still reminding women of the importance of having a man her life. It's sorta genius and I'm THINKING that I can do the same thing with my SMART GIRL RULES concept.

2:30pm

SMH... Joan is never going to be able to replace me. This afternoon's candidates sucked. The first two were both under dressed and unimpressive and the last candidate

— Tim's niece — just talked too damn much and her voice was annoying.

7:42pm
Meeting Cindy at her place to go over the shower stuff.

Friday, October 19th
7:26am
Lying in bed thinking. I'm feeling overwhelmed. After seven interviews; none of the candidates are a good fit and the thought of leaving Joan with somebody who sucks - SUCKS. Secondly, Cindy and her dating lectures are stressing me the eff out. Last night, she continued to ply me with take-out, martinis, and her brainwashing banter.

2:15pm
Last minute interview and the candidate is fifteen minutes late. She was supposed to be here at two.

2:22pm
She just arrived.

2:30
It was short and sweet. The poor girl, Marissa was her name. She didn't stand a chance as Joan wasn't having it. She walked her out and on her way back in, she yelled out to me, "Miss Alexa, you are the only girl in my life who can get away with being late and you know it."

I yelled back, "I know Joan, I'm a lucky girl."

Saturday, October 20th
12:27pm
Going to the gym and then meeting Madelyn for brunch.

6:01pm
Brunch was an effin blast and we had a last minute plus one. We met a cool ass chick named Cassandra when

194

Madelyn and I where in the bathroom. She's a tall mixed chick with sandy brown curly hair and great style. She told us her date flaked so we invited her to sit with us.

7:11pm
Finally I'm home and going to bed. We all split a cab uptown and I was the last stop. I have a massive headache from all of the mimosas, but it was worth it. It's always nice to meet another cool ass girl.

Sunday, October 21st
12:12pm
I just received a text message from Cassandra. She invited both Madelyn and I to a restaurant tasting this evening. I replied yes, but Madelyn can't swing it.

6:51pm
On the way out. I need to be downtown by eight.

8:03pm
I just arrived and it's packed. It's a Mediterranean restaurant and the decor is awesome. I spot Cassandra and she looks super cute. She's soo working the crowd and when our eyes finally lock we both start laughing.

9:45pm
So here's the deal. Great girls hang out with great girls and on my way to the bathroom I have an epiphany. Cassandra will take my place at the brokerage firm. She's perfect. Smart, savvy, and cool. Joan will love her and as they say, I'm paying it forward. I'm going to offer her my old job with Joan just like Liv offered me her old job with Kelly.

10:00pm
Again, it was de-ja vu. We just ordered a round and this time she was the one who jumped up with excitement and spilled the drinks. I told her about the position and she's totally interested.

Monday, October 22nd

8:45am
Joan will be in around nine-thirty and the minute she arrives, I'm going to tell her about Cassandra.

9:49am
YAY!! Joan wants to meet with her for lunch today. I'm calling now and I hope she can make it.

10:01am
Cassandra returned my call and she's available.

12:33pm
Cassandra arrived early and obviously she and Joan hit it off because they've been in her office for nearly an hour.

1:00pm
I ended up ordering in. Joan offered her the job and she accepted so now we are having a working lunch.

3:00pm
Coffee break. Cassandra is now doing the flyin' and as she walks out; I yelled out to her, "Ask for Johnnie and tell him you're the NEW ME."

3:02pm
My phone is buzzin'. It's Kola.

3:05pm
I answered. He wants to come over and I told him yes. I've been ignoring my feelings. Every time he's called or sent a text I've wanted to answer. I need to see him. Being able to tell Jacobson exactly how I felt last week was good for me and I need to do the same with Kola.

6:00pm
No gym tonight. I'm going to Bloomingdales. My gift cards are burning a hole in pocket and I want to get something cute to wear for the baby shower.

8:58pm
Just got in and received a text from Kola.

SEXY LEXI. BE THERE SOON AND BRINGING FOOD FOR YOU.

9:35pm
I know Kola is on his way, but I haven't moved. I'm not my usually frantic self. I'm on the couch snacking on my leftovers from lunch. I'm actually hungry and need a head start on dinner because I can only eat soo much of his hot spicy food. The apartment is a tad bit messy and I really need to freshen up, but I'm not. When he arrives, he's just going to have to be okay with the girl who opens the door.

10:27pm
He's here. I'm buzzing him up.

10:30pm
When I open the door, Kola greets me with a big kiss on the lips and then pulls out a bouquet of roses that he's hiding behind his back. He passes me the flowers, drops the food that was in his other hand and grabs my waist and pulls me tight.

The flowers are getting crushed and I begin to speak, but he interrupts, "Alexa, I love you. I want you to know, that I really do love you, Lexi."

My heart begins to beat hard. My eyes tear up. I drop the flowers and hug him even tighter. That's all I've ever really wanted to know. I miss him and we've spent soo much time together having fun that I haven't been able to rationalize the idea of just erasing him from my life. I know that we will probably never have anything serious, and that's okay because his actions tonight proved why I like him soo much.

11:15pm
My mouth is on FIRE. I couldn't help it. I had to taste the food. It's spicy, but frickin good.

Tuesday, October 23rd

12:29am

Kola just left. After we ate, we had a few glasses of wine. He invited me to come downtown with him, but I declined. My emotions are running high and I want to stay in and write.

2:01am

I didn't write shit. Just woke up on the couch. Moving to the bed.

8:30am

The train is packed and I didn't get a seat. I'm pissed.

8:45am

At 96th street and finally people are getting off. I plop down in an open seat and pull out my paper and can't help but notice the girl sitting next to me. She's crying. Not loud, but I see her tears. I wish I had tissue to give her, but don't. We've reached the next stop and there's no way I can ignore what I see. I lean over and ask her if she's okay.

8:55am

DEATH TO ALL BOYS!!! I'm ready to stab Mark and I've never even meet him. By 50th street, Jennifer, told me her entire story. She's devastated and rightfully so. She was misled and betrayed. We both are getting off at the next stop; as we gather our things, she wipes her tears. I look at her and tell her that she must pick her last day to cry, as she can't be this sad for the rest of the year. She looks up and tells me I'm right. I tell her that maybe it's not today or even next week, but at some point she has to stop with the tears. And then it hits me:

SMART GIRL RULE #8

PICK YOUR LAST DAY TO CRY

She hands me her card and I promise to stay in touch and when I turn to walk away, I too wipe away a tear because I know I have to follow my own rules.

9:15am
Cindy called. She wants to grab lunch. She's in a frenzy about the shower and wants to go over a few more things. What? I don't know, but I told her that she's paying.

9:30am
Cassandra just arrived. She's going to be in the office a few days this week and then next week she starts.

1:00pm
Cindy's here. We're off to lunch.

2:16pm
I'm back and didn't drink nearly enough. Like any expectant mother, Cindy is super excited and she wants everything to be perfect for her shower. We went over the guest list twice, the flower arrangements and seating chart twice and every other thing she could think of twice. Not to mention, in-between going over the shower details she slipped in her usual pep talk regarding my love life. She thinks it's time for me to just pick a guy and settle down. We've been friends for years and she believes that there have been some good guys that I pushed to the left in favor of some not soo good guys. She thinks I'm being too picky and should just learn to love the next boy that's all over me.

2:50pm
Joan is meeting with Cassandra to brief her on a few things and I'm dipping into one of the conference rooms to write.

Tuesday at 3

"Settle"

It's such a nasty word as it holds a lopsided truth that leaves one party feeling slighted. It resonates defeat. It's like telling a proud athlete to throw the game. A true warrior — even when faced with imminent loss — will never succumb.

Thus, SETTLING is not an option. It just isn't and I can't.

3:10pm
Kola called, but I didn't answer. I wanted to, but realize that I must put him on ice. He was truthful yes, but I know that even though he expressed his love for me, it isn't enough. I need more.

Thursday, October 25th
9:08am
I'm late, but not worried because I know Cassandra is going to be early.

9:31am
I'm in and just received a text from Kelly. She wants to know if I can come down to the new office tomorrow. She wants to introduce me to the team and I need to fill out some paperwork. This all works out great because Joan has a short day and Cassandra isn't coming in.

Friday, October 26th
12:04pm
The morning breezed by and I'm getting outta here by one.

1:15pm
I'm on the way to the new office and I can't believe it.

1:48pm
I'm lost. Soho can be tricky and I can't read a map or follow directions to save my life.

2:04pm
I'm here and soo excited.

2:09pm
I'm still here waiting. I've buzzed the door a million times and no one is buzzing me back.

2:12pm
Liv answered and I have five flights of stairs until I get to the top.

2:14pm
When I reach the fourth floor I pull myself together.
Everyone preaches don't judge a book by its cover but
everybody does.

2:15pm
The door opens and Liv greets me with a hug. I peer
down the hall and realize that the office is actually
a two-bedroom apartment Kelly has converted. The
walls are slate gray and the furniture is a soft blue.
The walls are covered with framed magazine clippings
and miscellaneous artwork. It's very corporate chick.
We pass the kitchen area and I peep in. It's about
the same size as mine, but with all stainless steel
appliances and a small table. We keep walking and
reach what would be the first bedroom, except it's the
first office space. There are two desks and a hand
painted mural on the wall that looks like a ghetto
forest. It's awesome — very abstract with graffiti and
trees. Liv stops and tells me that her desk is to the
left and the other desk belongs to Gabrielle who I met
at the AM magazine party early in the year.

We keep walking and enter an open space that would
be the living room, but instead it's a workspace with
four desks, a couch and cute table that has chairs that
neatly fit into place.

Liv re-introduces to me to Regina who I also met at the
AM Party and then a new girl, Traci. Then she points to
the empty desk and tells me that it's mine and I smile.
We keep walking and finally reach a closed door. Liv
opens it and it's Kelly's office. She's on the phone,
but behind her I see it all. The name of the magazine
and its tag line cover the wall. It's front and center
in big block letters:

D.E.F.I.N.I T.I.O.N

"what it means is up to you"

She smiles and waves. Liv is to my right and I reach out and pinch her arm. She looks at me and says, "Ouch, why the pinch?"

I reply, "Because I'm dreaming, effin dreaming."

2:25pm
Kelly just popped out and announced that she wants all of us to gather in her office in five minutes.

2:30pm
All five of us are in Kelly's office, but she's still on the phone. She looks up and mouths, "One minute." When she hangs up, she stands up and comes over to me and then says, "Everyone this is Alexa Ross. She's the final piece to our puzzle and together, we all are going to do great things."

5:00pm
After our group meeting, I spent some one on one time with Kelly and the rest of the afternoon with Liv going over my new daily tasks. My first day at the magazine is Tuesday, November 6th and I'm pumped.

5:30pm
Liv and I are grabbing a drink and then I'm taking the train uptown and she's meeting a guy for dinner.

7:45pm
I'm home and in for the rest of the night. Cindy's shower is on Sunday and I'm going to take it easy until then.

11:47pm
I fell asleep on the couch and awoke to three missed calls from Cindy.

Saturday, October 27th
12:01am
Ay dios mio! (Translation — Something bad just happened) Cindy is stressed. According to the news,

a big storm is headed towards the city and she thinks that attendance to the shower will be impacted, but I assure her that the media inflates things and everything will be fine.

10:03am
Again, just hung up with Cindy. She was right. This storm is real and she's freaking out. Both her dearest friends and closest family members were all planning to fly in, but the airlines have already started canceling flights.

11:47am
One the way to gym and then going to meet Cindy and her sister Paige at her apartment.

2:13pm
I dare not say Ay dios mio again, but **Ay dios mio again**. The storm is crazy and it's named after a girl, Hurricane Sandy. I'm stopping to grab some take-out and wine. Cindy can't drink, but Paige and I are going to need something.

5:14pm
We've reached out to everyone on the guest list requesting that they get back to us ASAP regarding their attendance and so far only 50% of the guests are going to "try" to make it. John, Cindy's husband, is glued to the TV and it's obvious that the city is slowly moving towards a complete shut down. This storm is serious.

6:15pm
Cindy is crying and John is trying to calm her down.

6:25pm
Paige just ran out to grab more wine as we are about to throw a *pity party*. We are going to have to cancel the shower and it sucks.

9:15pm
I'm headed home. John put Paige and me in a taxi. We reached out to the girls and with John's help have decided that we will still give Cindy the best shower ever. John was only able to get half of the deposit back from the venue. But under the circumstances, they are willing to prepare a small sampling of every food item that was ordered and will package it so we just have to pick it up. The cake is still a go so Ava will grab it first thing in the morning and Madelyn is bringing balloons and flowers. Lastly, Liv and I are meeting up at noon so we can pick out gifts. We want Cindy to have presents to open.

10:15pm
John called. He is going to come up with an excuse to get Cindy out of the house tomorrow and then when she returns, her surprise baby shower will await her.

Sunday, October 28th
9:00am
Operation Surprise! is in full effect. We had a conference call this morning and all of us are clear on our duties.

9:45am
John sent a text and he's taking Cindy shopping. They're leaving in two hours and I sent him a text back and told him to somehow convince her to wear white. He replied:
> 8½ MONTH PREGNANT WOMAN WEARING WHITE IN
> OCTOBER ON THE EVE OF CATEGORY THREE STORM.
> YEAH RIGHT.

I replied:
> LOL.. OK AT LEAST GET HER TO WEAR A WHITE
> BLOUSE.

He replied:
> THAT'S MORE LIKE IT. SEE YOU GIRLS LATER.
> BTW- IT WAS ANNOUNCED THAT THE SUBWAY IS

SHUTTING DOWN TODAY AT 7:00PM SO I WILL CALL
CAR SERVICE SO YOU ALL GET HOME SAFE.

1:31pm
Cindy's apartment looks beautiful. As soon as they
left we all snuck in. Together, we transformed the
dining and living room into pure white bliss. There
are crystals hanging from the ceilings, white roses
and balloons cover every piece of space, and her gifts
are immaculately wrapped with intertwined pink and
blue satin ribbon. The food table looks delectable and
her three-tier butter-cream frosting cake with fresh
flowers cascading down the center is magazine worthy.
The lights are out and we've lit candles so when the
doors open she will be shocked.

1:36pm
John just sent a text. They are on the way up.

1:41pm
We can hear John and Cindy in the hallway. He's telling
her that his phone is buzzing so he wants her to unlock
the door. The key turns and when the door opens we all
yell "Surprise."

1:44pm
Cindy is still standing at the door. She's crying.
I'm crying. Ava is crying. Madelyn is crying. Liv
is crying. Paige is crying. There have been many
occasions where we all have demonstrated the lengths
that we are willing to go to prove our commitment to
our friendship and today is one of those days.

4:04pm
We're hammered – John included – and we are all
cracking up because we think Mommy Cindy is feeling a
little loopy herself. We convinced her to have a glass
of champagne in honor of today's celebration and after
a fifteen-minute call with her OBGYN, she agreed.

206

Monday, October 29th
9:00am
I'm home. Joan called and told me not to come in. I
called Cassandra and delivered the same message.

9:00pm
This storm is beyond serious. Both the Jersey Shore
and Coney Island have been virtually obliterated. The
level of devastation keeps mounting. The neighborhoods
in the city uptown aren't affected, but everyone who
lives south of thirty-third street is royally screwed
and this includes Madelyn. She's on her way to my
apartment now.

Tuesday, October 30th
9:01am
I'm home. Joan called this morning and told me not
to come in until Thursday. A few of her directs live
in Jersey and none of them have power. We went over a
few items so I do have a couple things to do. I called
Cassandra and let her know not to come in until Thursday.

9:17am
John sent a text. Cindy went into premature labor.

2:19pm
On what began as the prelude to one of the worst weeks
ever has lead us all to bare witness to our biggest
joy. The five of us are at the hospital as everyone
else; Cindy's and John's parents couldn't fly in. Liv
sent a text and wants a play by play because she's not
going to make it.

2:45pm
I'm back in the waiting room with pen and paper in
hand. In between contractions Cindy screamed out, "Oh
My Lord, **she's** kicking my butt" not realizing that she
had a slip of the tongue. She and John had been keeping
the sex of the baby a secret, but we all heard her and
began to beam with joy.

Tuesday at 3

"The It Girl"

There is something to be said about being the hottest girl in the room. The girl that everyone one wants to meet. The one that every boy wants to kiss.

She's time stamped, everyone remembers the minute she appeared.

Compliments come her way like air, and it never gets old.

She's special and knows it. And as she stays hamessed in her clever bliss; legs perfectly crossed and lips puckered, she commands respect without seeking.

For her, life is magic.

3:33pm
She's here!!

                    NOW PRESENTING:
              Miss Harlow Jordana Miles
              Seven Pounds, Five Ounces.

Our tears can't stop.

NOVEMBER

Friday, November 2nd

7:30am
I'm up early. It's my last day and I'm excited, but most of all, I'm proud. I've been preaching change in my life and I'm executing.

8:00am
It just hit me – I haven't called my boy-friend Michael, as he too will be proud.

8:30am
The trains are running slow. The city is in disarray and there are communities in the surrounding boroughs that are ruined. This storm has wreaked havoc on the tri-start area.

9:00am
Who effin knew?? I have a present sitting on my desk and it's from Tim.

9:09am
Again – Who effin knew? Obviously Joan told her directs that I accepted a job at a magazine because Tim gave me a Levenger pen, Niki gave me an amazing bucket handbag, and again Joan presented me with a gift card – except this time it wasn't to Home Depot, it was to the Spa at the Mandarin Oriental Hotel and the card read –

> *Alexa, A womans career helps to define her character. Do yourself another favor – continue to work on you – all of you.*
> *And in-between every meeting, every conference call find solace in possibly being the*

210

only woman in the room. At first you may feel intimidated, but by your third meeting, you will realize that it is you who owns the room.
   Trust me.
   I'm rooting for you.

                                    Joan

12:34pm
POWER LUNCH except the weights have been replaced with a medium rare rib-eye, mashed potatoes, and creamed spinach. I'm at lunch with Joan and her directs.

3:00pm
The baton has been passed. Cassandra is the new me and I'm the new Liv. I have an appointment for highlights at four so it's time to vámonos, but my last task of the day will be hardest. I have to say goodbye to Joan. I head towards her office and see that the door is shut, but I know she's not on the phone. I reach out to open the door and she sees me through the glass and jumps up. She smiles and I smile back and we both extend our arms for a hug, but then she quickly lets go and tells me to leave at once.

I squint my eyes and ask, "What's wrong?"

She replies, "We both agree that crying at the office is a big no-no so, Out! I'll have Cassandra schedule lunch for us in two weeks. Now Go! You're on the way to a very important appointment and we both know that under no circumstance would you ever be late for that."

As I walk out her office I stop and turn around and before I get a chance to speak, Joan pulls out a tissue to wipe away a tear and then says, "I'm going to miss you and you know it."

4:22pm
Just like Joan, my stylist Maria is over my antics and wants me to commit. While doing my highlights, she stops mid foil and announces that she is sick of my "black girl Jennifer Aniston cut" and wants to do something drastic.

5:01pm
Maria is removing the foils and after she washes my hair, she says she is making a change.

5:17pm
I'm out of the shampoo bowl and back in her chair on the cusp of change.

5:26pm
The snipping has begun and I can hear it, but dare not look.

5:36pm
Oh My God. My eyes have been closed and Maria just gave me the green light to look. I open my eyes and I'm frozen. I have bangs. She cut bangs.

6:07pm
My hair has been blown out and straightened. Everyone in the salon thinks I look great.

6:15pm
I'm starring in the mirror and it hits me, I'm about to be the NEW GIRL.

6:30pm
I'm walking down the street and using every opportunity that presents itself to look at the NEW ME. Every store front, car window, and slightest reflection.

Saturday, November 3rd
12:01pm
At the gym for a quick workout and then I'm swinging by Cindy's apartment to hang out with Miss Harlow.

212

2:01pm

When Cindy opens the door, she does a silent scream and mouths, "Bangs, you cut bangs." We hug and then she whispers in my ear, telling me the baby is sleeping so we have to be quiet until she wakes up.

4:01pm

Harlow is the best. She is one of the girls because she is proving to be soo chill. I'm sitting on the couch holding her and watching TV while Cindy and John lay down for a disco nap. I had to pressure them into it, as they are both full of exhausted joy and didn't want to be away from her for a second.

6:15pm

I was christened into Auntie-hood. Miss Harlow graced me with two shitty diapers and spit-up all over my shoulder.

6:47pm

On the train uptown and everybody is looking and it's not the stain from the spit up that has everybody's attention. It's the bangs. The mutha-effin BANGS!!! I love the bangs.

Sunday, November 4th

11:01am

Skipping the gym and meeting Ava, Madelyn, and Liv for brunch and then we all are going over to Cindy's apartment to hang out with Harlow. I didn't tell them about my new hair and I can't wait to show off.

1:30pm

I just arrived at the restaurant and see Madelyn. I sneak up behind her and tap her shoulder. She turns around and gasps and then screams, "I love your hair." We hold hands and start jumping like only girls do and then Ava walks up and she's like "Why are we jumping?" Then she gasps and says, "Your hair! I love it."

1:57pm
Liv is running late, but the three of us are wasting no time getting the party started. Ava got the first round in honor of my new job and Madelyn just bought the second round in honor of my new hair.

2:01pm
Liv sent a text and will be here in five minutes.

2:15pm
Third times a charm. Liv too loves the bangs and the third round was on her.

4:30pm
Brunch was great and we are all tipsy and really in no condition to play Auntie to baby Harlow, but we are all going anyway. We promised Cindy that we would bring her something to eat so we can't cancel.

8:00pm
I'm in. John is such a sweetie. Again, he arranged for car service for us.

Tuesday, November 6th
7:01am
Leaving the apartment now. I have to vote before I go to the office and can't be late on my first day.

9:00am
When I reach my desk, I see stacks and stacks of magazines and on top of the last stack is a hand written note:

Alexa take a look and make a list of all of the contributing editors. Ill explain more when I return. Well grab lunch.

9:29am
I'm still **BANGIN!!** Everyone in the office likes my hair.

12:59pm
I don't know who is talking more — me or Kelly. Her vision for this magazine is intense and I want in. I told her about my writing. I couldn't keep it from her.

2:29pm
Back at the magazine and it's such a different vibe. At the brokerage firm I had a cubical aka my fake office, but now I share an open space and my sins are just a little more visible.

2:59pm
About to write and gonna make it quick.

Tuesday at 3

"Next"

What's next?

My hope is that it will be everything that I've dreamed of.

Wednesday, November 7th
9:30am
I'm busy. Kelly presented me with a TO DO LIST of nearly twenty items that she needs completed by end of day.

4:30pm
I'm still busy. On her way out, Kelly swung by my desk. She thanked me for my work today and handed me a small box. I jokingly smiled and asked her if she was proposing and she replied, "Sorta, open it." I flipped up the top of the box and inside was a set of business cards. They read:

D.E.F.I.N.I T.I.O.N
M A G A Z I N E
ALEXA ROSS
212.555.7246

She then said, "I'm happy to have you here Alexa and I'm curious about your writing so have some samples on my desk by next week. I'm not back in the office until Friday, but we'll speak tomorrow."

6:30pm
No gym tonight. Traci and Gabrielle invited me to an event and another one on Friday. I'm beginning to realize that my new position requires my full commitment and my usual schedule of gym, boys, and writing will be altered a little.

Friday, November 9th
9:01am
Thank God Kelly is a coffee drinker. I'm at 'Bucks doing a coffee run for the office. This is my second time at the new location and I haven't made friends. Everyone is nice, but there's no Johnnie.

Saturday, November 10th
11:01am
I had fun last night at the event with Traci and Gabrielle. I passed out cards and one of the guys I met

called me. His name is Ray. He's a tall handsome Cuban dude. He works in graphic design at a music magazine. He wants to grab drinks on Monday.

Sunday, November 11th
3:00pm
Easy day. I went to the gym and now I'm at 'Bucks working on my assignment from Kelly. I need to put together a portfolio or booklet of sorts to present her. She said she wanted to see my writing and I have to deliver.

6:01pm
I changed location. I'm at the dive bar on the Upper Westside. As I'm going through my writing, I know that I have something good: My SMART GIRL RULES. My plan is to write them` down and present the list accompanied by small vignettes that convey the sentiment of each rule. I goggled short writing and the word vignette popped up so I'm using it. I'm thinking this is *hot shit* and I can introduce the SMART GIRL RULES as a column idea for the magazine.

7:05pm
Still at the bar and not leaving anytime soon. Not only have I ordered jalapeno poppers and cheese fries, I've compiled all of the rules I have so far:
SMART GIRL RULES

#1 LET THE GUY FALL IN LOVE WITH YOU BEFORE YOU FALL IN LOVE WITH THE GUY.

#2 NEVER CRY AT THE OFFICE.

#3 TRY TO ALWAYS LOOK NICE.

#4 GET YOUR ROCKS OFF DURING FOREPLAY.

#5 ALWAYS KEEP SUNGLASSES IN YOUR PURSE.

#6 BE A SMART GIRL.

#7 NEVER BE THE PENCIL IN BITCH.

#8 PICK YOUR LAST DAY TO CRY.

7:08pm
I'm short four rules and have to come up with the remaining ASAP. There will be twelve issues so I need twelve rules. I have to pitch this as if I'm a client or a prospective author who wants to be a contributing writer for the magazine.

8:08pm
On the train uptown and the next rule just popped in my head. As I pull out a piece of paper to write it down I start smiling.

SMART GIRL RULE #9
NO MORE FREE BJ'S

How could I forget this?

Monday, November 12th
9:01am
I've arrived at the office and Traci is my first hello. She's a chill white chick with a boyish haircut and ill style and I'm beginning to believe that she will always be the first face I see as Kelly's schedule is erratic and everyone else arrives around 9:30ish.

12:01pm
Going to the gym. I have a membership that allows me to workout all over the city and there's a location blocks away.

2:45pm
Just received a text from Ray and I soo dropped the ball. He wants to go to a listening party for a new artist and I would have totally worn something else, but thank goodness I happen to have a pair of wedges in my gym bag.

5:30pm
I'm outta here and going to grab a dress to wear tonight. Kelly left around three and I'm done for the day. I have to meet Ray by eight so I have plenty of time to pull it together.

8:20pm
The effin train. I'm late and what sucks is that I was actually on time. I've reached the lobby of the building and am definitely in the right place. It's packed with hip cool ass people and everyone is waiting for the elevator.

8:21pm
Just got a text and its Ray:
PRETTY-PRETTY WHERE R U??

I smile as I type my reply. The night we met, the first thing he said to me was, "Look at you — so pretty-pretty."

8:30pm
I'm upstairs and the place is packed with cool ass people.

11:01pm
What a fun night. Ray took a cab with me uptown and then we stopped and got pizza. He walked me to my apartment and wanted to come up, but I told him no. It wasn't super messy, but messy enough to not have new boy up and he was okay with that. We shared a quick kiss on the lips and he invited me to another event on Thursday.

Tuesday, November 13th
9:09am
My phone is buzzing. It's Ray.

10:47am
Just received text #5 from Ray since we spoke this morning and I'm too busy to reply. Each text is getting

mushier and mushier and as I read each one my soft snicker is turning into full laughter. He's in new girl euphoria. It's the phase that men go through when they first meet you. They are all over your ass and can't stop with the text messages, phone calls, and compliments.

11:15am
I finally replied to Ray's text and we're meeting for lunch at one-thirty and I need to pull it together before I head out. There's only one bathroom in the office space so I don't have the freedom that I did at the brokerage firm to pull myself together.

11:30am
Traci came over to my desk and asked for some info that Kelly had me print out and when I reached down to pull it out of the drawer, she saw my flat iron and make-up bag. She laughed at me. We were talking earlier this morning about hair – the ease of hers and the complication of mine.

12:10pm
Traci is now on the BFF list. She just dropped a laminated sign on my desk with suction grips on the back. It reads:
    BATHROOM IN USE – GIRL WITH COOL HAIR ON BOARD.

I LUV HER… The support I receive from women never gets old.

12:45pm
Thank God I'm not the only one in the office who had a lunch meeting. Kelly just left fifteen minutes ago; Regina, Liv, and Traci are leaving now and Gabrielle shut the door to her office. The bathroom is mine.

1:30pm
Perfect timing. I see Ray and he sees me.

2:31pm
I'm back at the office and I have another note from Kelly. Lunch was great, but I have no time to daydream. She's gone for the day and not only does she need me to be in at seven in the morning, she left me with another TO DO LIST. It's smaller than the last one, but it still needs to be done.

2:56pm
I have three seconds to write and then going in Liv's office to go over tomorrow's schedule.

Tuesday at 3

"Change"

It's scary, but good. Without it there's no evolution.

3:15pm
I have soo much to do.

7:31pm
Leaving the office now. Going to the gym then going home.

9:58pm
Just hung up with Ray. We're going out on Saturday.

10:11pm
Took a shower and now going to bed.

Wednesday, November 14th
5:15am
I'm up.

6:00am
On the train.

6:45am
Walking up the stairs to the office.

6:59am
Grabbing coffee with Traci.

7:31am
Leaving Kelly's office with notes in hand.

12:31pm
No gym. Grabbing lunch for the office.

6:31pm
Not leaving anytime soon. I'm starting on tomorrow's tasks today.

10:31pm
Finally home and going straight to bed. I have a missed call from Ray, but I'm too tired to respond. I'm sending him a text telling him we'll talk tomorrow.

Thursday, November 15th
9:00am
Again today will be busy. Kelly has a lunch meeting with the group that invested in the magazine and she wants me to attend.

9:30am
Coffee run and I finally made a friend – the new Johnnie. His name is Kyle and he is just as fabulous.

2:30pm
The lunch meeting was unreal and now I know exactly what Joan meant when she said it is you – the girl – who owns the room. As I sat at the table, I watched Kelly. She spoke and the investors, all boys, hung on to her every word.

5:00pm
Kelly is gone for the day. At lunch, she not only introduced me as her assistant, but as a possible contributing writer. As soon as I'm outta here, I'm hitting the gym and then going to a restaurant in the neighborhood to eat dinner and work on my column proposal. I put myself on her schedule tomorrow at five.

9:37pm
My proposal is done and I feel good, but I can't come up with any more rules.

Friday, November 16th
10:39am
It's finally coffee time. My new position is no joke and there's no room for "ass-ing" around.

12:31pm
At the gym and on the treadmill multitasking. I sent Ray a text and in between sprints I'm doing arm sets with barbells.

2:30pm
Ray replied and we're meeting for Saturday brunch.

3:13pm
Kelly wants to have a group meeting in ten minutes.

3:33pm
There is a GOD, but there's also a CAVEAT. I now have one more day to see if I can come up with the remaining SMART GIRL RULES because Kelly wants us all to come in tomorrow by nine. Next week is Thanksgiving so we will loose two days and the final mock up for the first edition has to be ready by the 4th.

8:00pm
I can't come up with any more rules to save my life and just called Michael for help. He answered and as usual gave me sound advice. He told me not to worry, to be content with what I have and to present with the intent to supply more. Simple. He promised that we would connect after the holiday.

10:01pm
Just hung up with Ray. We killed tomorrow's brunch and will meet for dinner instead.

Saturday, November 17th
8:00am
On the way to the office.

8:45am
Stopping to grab coffee, as I'm sure everybody will need it.

8:53am
Great minds think alike. Turns out Traci stopped and grabbed croissants and muffins and just sent a text asking that I hit 'Bucks. I replied:
                    IN LINE NOW!! ☺

11:30am
Going in to deliver my pitch for the column.

12:01pm
In the bathroom breaking SGR #2 - DON'T CRY AT THE OFFICE. Kelly said YES! The column is a go. She explained to me that the deliverable time is actually several weeks before the issue goes to print; therefore, I have several months to come up with the last three rules.

12:06pm
Back at my desk and I'm soo happy.

3:00pm
Heading home now and have to come back tomorrow at nine. Kelly isn't playing around with the magazine. The first issue has to be perfect.

9:01pm
I'm late. The subway service was terrible tonight because of rail repairs. I sent Ray a text, but he didn't reply.

9:21pm
I'm finally here and see Ray at the bar.

9:31pm
I could tell Ray was a li'l pissy because I was late so I offered to buy the first round.

10:30pm
Ray is still pissy but now less "pissy mad" and more "pissy drunk." We decided to remain at the bar and have dinner instead of getting a table and the drinks never stopped. I'm always shocked when I realize that I can actually handle my liquor better than a guy.

11:30pm
On the way home. Ray wanted me to come over to his place, but that wasn't happening. There is no way that

I could show up to the office in the morning looking like last night. Kelly is no fool and neither am I for that matter. I'm taking this new position very seriously as I really think I've found my niche. I like writing.

Sunday, November 18th
8:50am
Made it to the office and when I walk in, I realize that I'm the last to arrive. Kelly, Traci and Gabrielle are working and immediately tell me to drop my bag and help. They've pushed our desks together to make one big table and each page of the magazine is spread out in numerical order, spilling out onto the floor. Liv and Regina are in Kelly's office and yell out a synchronized, "Hi, Alexa. You're late." As I bend down, Traci hands me a blank page that's marked with a big yellow post-it note that says **PAGE 46**. She tells me to follow the order and continue to place each page down in the landscape position as she hands it to me.

9:14am
Kelly is now on the phone and I use this opportunity to whisper in Traci's ear. I lean over and say, "I thought she said to be here at nine?" Traci whispered back, "She did, but we'll talk later. Just keep putting the pages down."

9:35am
Breakfast run and as Traci and I walk out, Kelly yells, "Alexa, when it's game time, we all lace up. There's no bench warmers at **D.E.F.I.N.T.I.O.N**. Traci will fill you in."

I smile, while saying, "I gotcha."

10:37am
When we reach the bottom of the steps, I look at Traci, bugging my eyes out and ask, "What the hell?? She said be here at nine and I was here like ten minutes before nine."

Traci laughs while pushing the door to the building open. She turns around, grabbing me by the shoulder and

228

says, "Alexa, grow the fuck up. If this is what you want to do with the rest of your life then put your heart in it. I've seen you totally be prepared for a date twice now, so put that same thought into your career."

1:35pm
We worked through breakfast and now we are working through lunch.

3:05pm
All done and THANK GOD. There is no way I could have made it through today hung over. I'm soo glad I had the wherewithal to cut myself off last night.

3:17pm
Walking into Kelly's office to say goodbye, and as I enter, she tells me to close the door and have a seat. She takes a sip of water then goes right in, "Alexa. I'm running a business — my business — and if you aren't up to the challenge then your time will be short here. The Thanksgiving holiday is approaching and although I'll be working, I want the group to take this upcoming time to recharge. The office will close at noon on Wednesday and when I see you on that following Monday, I expect to see a new dedicated you."

I replied, "I will be here."

She let out a smile and continued. "Also, I will want to see the first proof of your column in its entirety. That means the layout, typesetting, and graphics — etcetera. If you remember, there was a blank page in the mock-up - PAGE 46. That's yours if you own it. You have all the resources right here in the office so use them. Until then, I'll see you in the morning bright and early."

Her phone rang, but before answering, she looked at me and again said, "Bright and Early - are we clear?"

And again, I smiled and replied, "I gotcha."

3:23pm
Just hung up with Ray. I'm going over to his house and bringing take-out and wine. I need him.

4:15pm
Ray's apartment is giving man-cave at its finest. He has the super big TV, pool table, nice leather couch, and the pièce de resistance: this cool ass small see through fridge, stocked with everything from champagne to beer, that serves as an end table. I love his place.

6:15pm
While we ate and drank, I told him about my day at the office. He assured me that he would help with the page layout and explained the importance of putting my best foot forward. He's been in the publishing industry since graduating from college and was just promoted to Senior Creative Designer. He reminded me how lucky I am to have such a coveted position. He remarked that if the magazine takes off and I have a column, my name would be associated with one of the most glamorous and prestigious industries.

7:15pm
We're on the couch cuddled up and the old me would have definitely opted to have a few more cocktails and plan to spend the night, but I can't. I have to go home. It's obvious I need to be in at eight in the morning instead of nine.

8:40pm
Ray put me in a taxi and I'm almost home.

9:21pm
Made it in. I called and thanked Ray for a great time and we are going to hang out later in the week.

Monday, November 19th
6:00am
I'm up.

8:00am
Made it the office and everyone is here. I'm early, but still technically late.

12:01pm
No lunchtime workout today. Actually, there will be no lunchtime workout all week.

8:00pm
Leaving the office and meeting Madelyn. She said she has a surprise.

9:03pm
"Cheerio." We are going to London, Baby!! Joshua aka #8 invited Madelyn and told her to bring a friend because he will be tied up in meetings while there and doesn't want her to be left alone.

9:15pm
We are wasting no time. Madelyn is on the phone with his assistant and they are setting up my trip. I told her that I could take any flight after twelve on Wednesday, but have to be back by Saturday night at the latest, as I can't afford to have any travel hiccups.

10:01pm
In a taxi going uptown. Madelyn wanted to stay out to celebrate our trip, and if I wasn't embarking on my new career in publishing I would have but alas, I can't.

10:49pm
Going to bed. I was on the phone with Ray telling him about my trip and asking him how I could get on his schedule before I get out of town. The good news is that he's going out of town too and we'll connect tomorrow and again when I return. He assures me that all I need to do is supply the content and he will put the rest together.

Tuesday, November 20th

7:45am
I'm at the office, but not before Traci. She still beat me.

8:15am
Kelly sent several emails and I'm soo glad I was here to respond. She will be in at nine and wants both coffee and today's TO DO LIST ready when she arrives.

10:15am
Today will be no joke. I've been in Kelly's office since she arrived and a lot of stuff has to be done.

12:31pm
Lunch run for the office and while I'm out I'm going to call Ray.

12:51pm
I'm back and as we all eat Kelly is throwing out more stuff that has to be done ASAP.

2:55pm
Kelly is on a call and I have ten minutes to write before I have to go back in her office.

Tuesday at 3

"My Voice"

My voice starts and ends with the truth.

It's strong.

It reflects my vision and helps to make my thoughts move.

Without paper, my voice would be alone.

It would have no showcase.

My voice is a piece of me.

My voice is the gateway to my smile.

My voice.

I have never been told to shut up.

Never been told to quiet down.

My voice is loud because my spirit is louder.

It is loud because I have been supported by many and discouraged by few.

My voice is the soundtrack to my life and today I'm turning the volume all the way up.

4:00pm
Madelyn sent an email with my itinerary. She's leaving tonight and I leave tomorrow. I'm on flight 7219 – JFK to LHR departs 9:30pm and arrives the next day at 9:25am. I return on Saturday night so this is great. I'm hoping I can go straight to Ray's to work on the column layout. While I'm gone, I'm going to mix business with pleasure and hopefully I'll be inspired.

4:09pm
I'm calling Ray right now. I need to know if he is available and down with my plan.

4:15pm
Ray's in! We're going to meet tonight. He has a few ideas that he wants me to think about while I'm on holiday. I'm amped.

6:01pm
Sent Ray a text. I'm not getting outta here until at least eight o'clock.

8:01pm
Leaving now and have to be back at the office at six-thirty sharp and I don't have a single complaint. I'm soo happy to finally have the career that I've always dreamed of.

8:02pm
Perfect timing. Ray called. He's grabbing take-out for us and I'm on my way.

9:37pm
Ray is about business. He had two digital proofs ready for me to look at when I arrived. Now, I just have to figure out which rule I want to start with and write something very powerful to accompany it.

10:59pm
Still at Ray's. We've transitioned from business to pleasure and he wants me to spend the night.

11:15pm
In the bathroom fixing my hair and I want to spend the night, but can't. There's no way I'm walking in the office looking like last night. I'm outta here.

11:30pm
Ray understood and put me in a taxi uptown.

Wednesday, November 21st
12:15am
Walking up the steps to my apartment and my phone is buzzing and I'm sure it's Ray.

12:59am
WRONG ANSWER. It was Kola and we've been on the phone ever since.

1:15am
Finally going to sleep. Tonight was the most time that we've ever spent on the phone and he was a very different guy. We talked about everything — EVERYTHING and he said he wants to see me soon and for once, I made no promises. I told him that right now, I'm focused on my new position and that maybe, if I have time, we can grab a drink during the next few weeks.

6:00am
On the way to the office and multi-tasking like a mutha. Every day, I've passed a cleaners as I've walked toward the office and this morning I grabbed a ton of stuff to drop off for same day cleaning. I will have no time to go shopping to grab new pieces for the trip, so I went "shopping" in my closest.

6:01am
Sent Traci a text and getting coffee and goodies for us.

6:20am
It's still just Traci and me and while we nosh, I pull out my laptop to show her my list of SMART GIRL RULES.

She thinks they are awesome, but feels that both the first and last rule need to be powerful. She reminded me – you only have one time to make a first impression.

8:23am
It's been non-stop since Kelly walked in. Everybody is busy.

11:54am
We're done! We've all shared hugs and "Happy Thanksgiving" wishes. It turns out that both Gabrielle and Liv need a mani/pedi too so we are heading to the nail shop together.

1:30pm
The nail shop is packed, but luckily we walked in at the perfect time and they were able to take all of us.

2:00pm
Liv and I are leaving while Gabrielle stays. Neither of us has the patience to sit there while our toes dry so we are hitting the city streets in flip-flops. It isn't too cold out, so our toes won't freeze.

2:10pm
My clothes aren't going to be ready until three o' clock, so Liv and I are going to grab lunch.

3:09pm
Lunch was great and it was my treat. I can't thank her enough for hooking me up with the job.

3:16pm
We exchanged air kisses and now we are on the move. She's going to get a blow out and I need to pick up my clothes and get home to pack and tidy up.

4:11pm
I'm home and I'm taking a disco nap. I just hit the wall. I'm tired.

5:15pm
No nap time for me. Madelyn called as soon as I closed my eyes and she is soo excited. Soo much so, that she arranged car service to take me to the airport and another car will be waiting for me when I land.

7:00pm
YAY!! I'm on the way to the airport and now I'm super excited.

7:45pm
The line to go through security is insane. I'm going to have to use my magic to cut to the front.

8:30pm
Ask and you shall receive... Not only did I get whisked through the line, but the agent also walked me into the airline lounge. I'm now enjoying a glass of champagne and reading a magazine.

9:30pm
It's time to take off!

Thursday, November 22nd
9:25am
I'm here! and my phone is buzzing. It's Madelyn. I knew she was sending a car to pick me up, but I didn't expect that she would come too.

9:45am
I see Madelyn and she's holding a sign with my name on it. I yell out to her in my *wanna-be* British accent, "Darling, Darling." When I reach her, she holds the sign up even higher and asks if I like it. I reply, "Of course I like it." She then clears her throat and says, "Alexa, look closely at the top right hand corner of the sign, and then tell me if you like it or do you love it?" And then I see it - a big sparkly diamond. Once again, we start jumping up and down like only girls do and I've added the sound track to our

excitement as I'm screaming, "You're engaged, you're engaged."

10:00am
Let the good times begin. No celebration is complete without some bubbly and Madelyn brought it. We are now in the back of the car toasting to the newly anointed **Mrs. Madelyn Abrahams**.

10:45am
We have been chatting and screaming nonstop since we got in the car. The good news is Madelyn warned the driver so he is taking it all in stride. I can't hear the details of her engagement story enough. She was totally surprised and Joshua spared no expense. He rented out an entire restaurant, filled it with roses and candles and when she reached their dining table, there was a box. She said he got down on one knee, fighting back tears, confessing that he hadn't met any other woman in his life who he felt that he couldn't be without — and she was that girl.

11:00am
We've finally reached the hotel and as we get out, Madelyn looks at me and now in *her* best British accent, says, "Bloody Hell, We've finally arrived. I know that you must be zonked." We both let out a big laugh because we know, that from this point forward, we'll be using our fake British accents and slang all weekend.

12:00pm
Madelyn just left my room and I'm going to bed. I was too excited to sleep on the plane so I definitely need a nap.

7:00pm
I'm up and getting dressed. We are going back to the same restaurant where Joshua proposed for a non-traditional Thanksgiving Dinner.

8:30pm
Better her than me. I'm upstairs in Madelyn and Joshua's suite and the new "Mrs." isn't ready yet so Joshua and I are going downstairs to the hotel bar for a drink.

9:01pm
Joshua is proving to be quite the wingman. As men approach, he quickly sways the conversation to me. His height and great looks a are dead giveaway that he's an athlete and even those who aren't familiar with American basketball are approaching to chat him up.

9:25pm
Madelyn made it and she is glowing and throwing up her left hand every five minutes. We decide to have one more drink before we head to the restaurant and it looks like we will be joined by one of Joshua's blokes. His name is Andrew, and per Madelyn, he's filthy rich.

11:00pm
We, which includes me, Madelyn, and Joshua, are amazed that the restaurant is totally thinning out. Andrew had to remind us that we weren't in NYC and that mostly every place else in the world closes at a ***proper*** hour.

11:16pm
Andrew is proving to be a total **WANKER** but I am a bit intrigued by how he made his fortune. I'm a changed girl, yes, but not stupid. It has to be nice to have at least one insanely rich contact.

11:30pm
Joshua's agent, teammates, and business partners have arrived and champagne bottles are popping and glasses are clinking as if his team won the championship game.

Friday, November 23ʳᵈ

12:00am

We are now having Madelyn's un-official engagement party. Joshua's agent and friends called a few people who then called a few people and the restaurant is busier now than it was during normal hours. While partying, Madelyn whispered in my ear and told me Joshua asked the owner to keep both the kitchen open and the staff on deck.

3:00am

London, Baby!!

6:09am

My head is pounding, my mouth is dry and as my eyes open, I look around and see that I'm not in my room. Even worse, I'm on the couch in Madelyn's suite lying next to Andrew. We are both fully dressed, and as I slide from under his grip, he wakes. He has to be still drunk, because he starts to grab me as if he wants me to stay. He's on some Austin Powers shit. He's slurring some cheeky gibberish.

6:15am

I found my handbag, shoes, and coat and got the hell outta there. I'm back in my room and set my alarm. I need to be up in forty-five minutes. I'm starving and that's when room service starts.

7:45am

Effin London. Where in the hell is the nearest McDonald's so I can get an egg mcmuffin?? Breakfast was sketchy. The menu only had traditional English breakfast and traditional English breakfast is sketchy.

3:15pm

I'm back upstairs in Madelyn and Joshua's suite and two of his teammates and Andrew are still there. We are all talking about last night and then it hits me, Madelyn and I nicknamed Andrew "MR W." and the joke was on his ass. He thought it stood for Mr. Wonderful, but it stands for Mr. Wanker.

3:45pm
Madelyn scheduled us for what will be my first real spa day this year. We are getting the works.

7:40pm
Madelyn and I feel soo good that we don't even feel like doing the transformation. I'm still in her suite. She wanted us to get dressed together so I brought all my stuff upstairs. We have one hour to make it happen.

9:05pm
Round Two... Joshua and I are having drinks in the hotel while we wait for Madelyn and he is still holding on to his wingman title. I've exchanged cards with three blokes one of whom will be in New York for the holidays and he said he would call.

10:00pm
Mr. W ended up joining us and tonight he seems to have taken the stick out of his ass. The four of us have all had one cocktail too many and our behavior is way to silly for the fancy restaurant that Madelyn chose for dinner.

11:31
Fancy Schmancy. Joshua is a successful guy and money is no object, but our dinner was not worth £500 pounds. We all are now tittering on being totally wasted and still starving. Mr. W knows a small Indian restaurant that will still be open where we can eat and smoke hookah.

12:31
Mr. W has redeemed himself. The food at the restaurant was good, smoking the hookah was fun, and now we are ready to party.

Saturday, November 24th
6:09am
My head is pounding, my mouth is dry, and as my eyes open, I look around and see that this time I'm in my room and wearing pajamas. This is good, but then I hear a familiar sound – someone gagging and the toilet flushing. *Ooh Lord* is what I think to myself.

I call out, in my fake British accent – "Darling, are you okay?" while not knowing who will answer.

And then I hear it, the real British accent, "Alexa dear, I'm legless, completely pissed and yet you and Madelyn… you both are brilliant and lovely girls, but you drink like sailors. How do you do it?"

I reply, "Mr. W you know girls are better than boys. Do you need help?"

He replies, "Dear, I'll manage, but please order something for us to eat."

7:45am
Ask and you shall receive… While Mr. W enjoyed his traditional English breakfast of questionable looking sausage, eggs and beans (I've never understood the Brits eating beans for breakfast) I managed to Americanize mine by ordering *à la carte*. I'm enjoying two eggs scrambled with bacon on wheat toast, coffee and OJ. **God Bless America.**

1:15pm
I'm up, but Mr. W is still sleep. Madelyn and I are grabbing lunch at the hotel restaurant and then I'm heading to the airport to catch the bird. My flight leaves at five o'clock.

4:45pm
I made it to the airport, breezed through the security line, and grabbed a ton of European Fashion magazines

242

to bring back to show Kelly. I also thought about Ray and picked up two magazines for him and sent him a text reminding him that I will see him later.

5:35pm
Up, Up, and Away!! NYC here I come.

8:30pm
I'm back! The flight was great, but we are still on the tarmac. There's traffic and no available gates for us to deplane and when I turn on my phone, I see that I too have major traffic on my phone. I knew for sure that I would receive a few text messages from Madelyn, and at least one from Ray, but had no idea that Mr. W would be blowing me the eff up.

8:45pm
Still on the plane and exchanging text messages with Mr W. He's all in his feelings about me not waking him up before I left to say goodbye. I reminded him — using Brit slang in my message — that he was a bloody, pissy mess and that I dared not wake him. He texted back and said that my face would have been a pleasant surprise. I sent a smiley face and he replied that he would ring me tomorrow.

9:04pm
Finally off of the plane and going straight to the loo, hoping that the queue won't be long. (*I'm still using British slang and will be for at least one more day.*)

9:30pm
I was so thrown by Mr. W.'s texts that I missed Madelyn's. She arranged for car service and they are calling now.

9:45pm
On the way to Ray's and he is ready to party. He wants to put off our work and go out for a late dinner and drinks. He believes that I have much more material than

I'm giving myself credit for and that we can knock it all out tomorrow.

10:39pm
I just lied to Ray. I told him I would be ready in thirty minutes, but it ain't happening. Traffic was a bloody miserable mess and I just arrived at his place.

11:39pm
I blew way past the thirty-minute mark and we're leaving now and Ray didn't budge. He let me do my whole transformation and didn't utter a single word.

Sunday, November 25th
12:15am
We were able to grab the last seating at this cute Italian place in the West Village and dinner has been the bomb.

1:15am
We are still out and have no plans of stopping anytime soon.

2:15am
We changed location and are now at a club in the Meatpacking District. We made friends with this cute couple from Spain and they invited us to sit at their table and the shots haven't stopped.

3:15am
We are partying our asses off.

4:15am
Partying is over and now it's time for breakfast.

5:15am
Breakfast is over and now its time to cuddle.

12:15pm
Cuddle time never happened. We both came straight in and passed out. Ray is still sleep and I'm sneaking out

to grab groceries. There's a store around the corner and he keeps his keys on a hook right next to the front door.

12:49pm
I'm back and he's still sleep and when he awakes, brunch will be ready.

1:45pm
Ray is up. The toilet flushed and he just yelled out that he wants to go get something to eat. I replied, telling him, "me too", but little does he know that when he walks in the living room, brunch awaits. Not only did I prepare an amazing meal, I bought flowers, fancy napkins, and champagne. I'm all about the presentation.

2:06pm
Brunch is cold, but I'm hot. When Ray walked in the living room he was surprised. I was sitting at the table and he came over, lifted me out of the chair, and carried me to the couch. He threw me down, pouncing on top of me declaring that the only thing he wanted to eat for breakfast was me.

3:00pm
According to Ray, today was the best brunch he ever had and I chimed in with a ditto. We still didn't do "it" but got very close. I just don't want to go there. The old me would have already done it, probably going as far as to break SGR #9 by giving him a BJ, but this NEW ME, the girl who is trying to stick to CHANGE, just can't.

5:59pm
Ray was right. It took no time to finish. The digital proof is done and looks amazing, but I secretly feel that the text that I've written lacks strength. As bad as, I want to stay and hang out, I'm leaving. I need go, drop my bags and then go back out to work.

6:31pm

Ray put me in a taxi and as I stare out the window I'm thinking. Traci was right. I only have one time to make my first impression. I not only need to write something new, I need to come up with a new rule. One that will show who I am as a writer, and everything that this column stands for.

11:55pm

I'm home and happy with what I have so far. It's not complete, but I'm glad I went out to work because I came up with the rule that speaks to the premise this column is built on:

SMART GIRL RULE #1

OWN YOUR WOMANHOOD

Monday, November 26th

7:00am

On the way out. I'm not sure what time Kelly expected me to be at the office, but I'm figuring eight o'clock is a safe start.

7:55am

When I walk in, I'm greeted with a playfully, but unanimous, "Alexa." Kelly and Traci were in the open work space again with all of the pages spread across the desks and floor.

Kelly, looked up and said, "Hand it over." I explained to her that I had a last minute change and that I needed to print out the latest and the greatest.

8:18am

Both Kelly and Traci had a lot to say. They like where I'm going, but hate the color scheme, font, and graphics. Ray made a caricature of me. It's a girl who's sitting at a desk with a pen and they think it lacks complexity and sophistication. However, Kelly is impressed that I delivered and let me in on a secret. Today's deadline was a test, the final is due next

Tuesday and after hearing all the changes I was going to have to make, I'm so happy. I just knew I would be up all night trying to finish this.

8:23am
Doing the coffee run and as I exit, Traci comes up behind me and playfully whispers in my ear, "Alexa – don't worry, I'll help you with the final draft. I'm glad to see that you are growing the fuck up."

I smile and as I pull the door closed, I call out to Traci; and when she turns around I flip her the bird. We both start laughing.

12:22pm
Busy morning. I'm hitting the gym for a run.

1:15pm
On my way back to the office and replying to a text from Mr. W. He wants to chat tonight.

6:15pm
On the way home. No gym tonight. I'm getting take-out in the neighborhood and then going to relax.

7:45pm
Talk, Talk, Talk... Mr. W has an opinion on everything and he is throwing cheap shots at both Madelyn and I and I don't like it. I'm getting off the phone. He was nicknamed Mr. W for a reason, yet I'm engaging him as if I forgot.

9:15pm
Talk, Talk, Talk... Now it's Ray who has as opinion on everything. The guy who just yesterday was so happy to have "me" for breakfast is now throwing me under the bus. I told him about the new rule and the changes that Kelly wants me to make and he unleashed a litany of underhanded jabs at not only me, but all women in the

publishing world. Until now he didn't have a nickname, but tonight he is turning into Mr. H - for "hater."

10:13pm
Going to bed, but thinking about the verbal beating I received from both Andrew and Ray. I've revoked their nicknames because I don't think I want to ever speak to either of them again. I'm in a good place and don't need any guys in my life who don't have my best interest at heart.

Tuesday, November 27th
6:00am
I'm up, but need ten more minutes. I'm hitting snooze.

6:05am
I can't get back to sleep because my phone is still buzzing. When I reach down, I see it's four missed text messages — three from Andrew and one from Ray — both cryptically trying to apologize for their comments last night.

11:49am
The morning breezed by. Kelly has a lunch meeting and I'm going to the gym for a Spin class.

1:30pm
The boys are back at it. Andrew just sent a text and Ray just called. I'm replying to neither.

2:30pm
Kelly sent an email. She's out for the rest of the day and wants me in tomorrow at seven.

2:59pm
It's time to write.

Tuesday at 3

"LMFAO"

Call me a feminist because I'm soo tired of men talking shit. Acting as if they know what it's like to be us. Pretending to walk in our shoes and move in our triumph. They couldn't be us on our worst day. Yet, they point fingers and claim to know what we feel. Betting on which of us are the unhappiest and testifying about what they believe we are all doing wrong.

It's all rubbish.

6:00pm
On the way home to relax. I need one more day to decompress and collect my thoughts. I haven't returned any of Andrew's or Ray's calls or texts, nor have I worked on the column.

Wednesday, November 28th
7:00am
I'm here.

7:30am
Coffee run and Liv's coming with me.

10:15am
Doing a second coffee run and Traci is coming with me. We have visitors. Kelly hired freelancers to assist with the project.

12:55pm
Lunch run, but I'm going by myself. I'm using this fake alone time as an opportunity to return both Andrew's and Ray's messages. I'm calling them both.

1:17pm
Andrew and Ray – what idiots. Boys can be soo silly. They both admitted to acting like jerks, and I appreciate their honesty, but I'm OVER IT.

Friday, November 30th
6:00pm
TGIF! What an effin week. I'm outta here. I'm going uptown to work on the column and then going to bed, as Kelly wants us back in the office tomorrow.

DECEMBER

Saturday, December 1st
9:00am
I stayed up late last night working on the final draft and it was totally worth it. Traci loves it and now we are working on a new graphic and type setting. Kelly had a last minute emergency and won't be in until ten.

1:00pm
Breaking for lunch and Kelly is treating all of us. I suggested the Mediterranean restaurant where Ray and I met for lunch. The food was good.

2:30pm
We are back to the office and back to work.

3:30pm
I talked up Ray. He just called, but I didn't answer. I really don't know what to say. I know he was just being a stupid boy, but frankly, I'm tired of stupid boys.

5:30pm
Ava sent a text and wants to do Sunday Brunch with the girls.

5:45pm
It's on! Everyone is coming, even Cindy.

Sunday, December 2nd
10:00am
Going to the gym and then getting a mani/pedi. Ava sent a text and we have a two o'clock reservation.

1:30pm
On the way downtown in a taxi. I didn't feel like taking the subway today and neither did Liv so I asked the driver to stop so we could pick her up.

2:01pm
On our way, Liv asked if Cassandra was coming and then it dawned on me that I hadn't reached out to her or Joan for that matter so I sent them both a text. Joan replied and will check her calendar then get back to me, and I'm hanging out with Cassandra on Friday.

3:30pm
The surprises keep coming. Ava is having a dinner party next Sunday and she wants us to get fancy. She's been dating a new guy and things are getting serious. He's also a partner at her firm and she wants us all to meet him.

4:00pm
Brunch is over, but my pity party is in full swing. Ava's dinner party is couples only and I have no one to invite so now both Liv and Madelyn are at the bar recruiting guys to be my date.

5:00pm
The day is over for Cindy and Ava, but Madelyn, Liv, and I are just getting started. Long Live the Party Girls!!

Monday, December 3rd
11:45am
Everyone is busy. The final mockup of the magazine is due tomorrow.

1:01pm
Traci and I are dotting the i's and crossing the t's on the column as I have to go in and show Kelly the final proof.

1:45pm
I'm back in the bathroom with tears in my eyes. Kelly loved it. She had a few minor changes, but thinks that the SMART GIRL RULES concept is great and has numerous ideas on how we can take it even further.

Tuesday, December 4th
8:00am
Four hours to T-minus and counting. The final mock up is being sent out at noon.

3:00pm
No need to write today, as I'm preparing to do my first reading. The final mock-up is complete and we are sipping wine and having an impromptu celebration. We all worked our butts off and since I'm the NEW GIRL, Kelly wants me to read the piece that I wrote for the January issue.

SMART GIRL RULES
Your 12 Commandments for 2013
By Alexa Ross

SGR #1

OWN YOUR WOMANHOOD

Strong. Resilient. Empowered. Trendsetting. Trailblazer.

All words used to describe WOMEN. Yet on the journey to reach these heights, sometimes we're faced with incredible lows.

We see our male counterparts, moving and shaking like it's nobody's business. We witness that for THEM manipulation is an afterthought and regrets — hell, in their world, there are none. Lying about everything from last year's earnings to extramarital affairs, each move is fueled by sex, money, and power. Each step calculated. We begin to compare stripes, fantasizing about this freedom. We can't help but to contemplate joining the boys club.

Is it really worth it? While it all sounds deceitfully pretty, you know that's not our path.

Men concentrate on their agendas all day, every day, while we quite often put our needs on the back burner. Enough. We women must learn to be committed to our own needs — no exceptions.

Woman is the most precious being on the planet. We hold the key to life. It is *our* world – with or without: husband, partner, lover, kids, career, house, car, clothes, money or jewelry. We don't need any of it to validate us. Our womanhood is the truth.

We cry. We yell. We hurt. These actions — validate and give voice to our feelings. These actions are part of our growth. And we deserve to grow.

We must stay SMART and remain committed to our own success — on our own terms. To embrace the scratches, because we know how to insure there will be no visible scars.

You are magnetic energy. So in charge the mirror can't even handle it. You know what you want. Stop waiting for permission. Go get it.

SMART GIRL RULE #1.
WOMANHOOD — own it.

Wednesday, December 5th
12:49pm
On the treadmill and six minutes into my run I realize that I'm bored with my workout regime. I continue, but as I hit my next stride, it clicks. I must continue to extend the change in my life. I've made changes with my look, my career and my love life, and now it's time to make changes to my workout routine. I'm amped and I'm going to finish my run, but tomorrow, I'm going back to Bikram yoga.

Thursday, December 6th
5:04pm
On the way to the gym. I can't start Birkam yoga today, as my hair will be a shitty ass mess. Liv invited me to grab drinks with some guys who work in P.R. and I need to be ready by eight.

11:39pm
Drinks turned into dinner and dinner could have turned into a nightcap with Liv, Samuel and Ian, but I got the hell out of there. Ian was all over me, but I could tell that he was just looking for Ms. Tonight and I need a guy who wants Mrs. Forever.

11:59pm
Goodbye kisses were exchanged and cab money was passed. I'm outta here.

Friday, December 7th
12:31am
In a taxi uptown and I did the inevitable. I sent Kola a text.

1:01am
I'm in and Kola didn't send a reply and even though I miss him, it is probably a good thing that he didn't get back to me.

10:30am
At the office and on cruise control. Kelly sent an email, she's working from home today.

5:30pm
Still no yoga. After the gym, I'm meeting Cassandra for drinks.

10:55pm
Drinks turned into dinner and dinner could have turned into a nightcap with Cassandra, Miguel, and Carlo, but I got the hell out of there. Tonight it was Carlo who was all over me, but I could tell that he was just giving me the Colombian version of last night. He too was just looking for "una puta para pasar el tiempo" (aka Ms. Tonight) and I need a guy who wants "Mi Mujer" (aka Mrs. Forever).

11:45pm
I'm home and my phone is buzzing. It's Ray, but I'm not answering.

11:55pm
My phone is buzzing again. It's Kola, but I'm not answering. I know I have some nerve as yesterday I was the aggressor but still — I'm not answering.

Saturday, December 8th
6:30am
What the Bloody Hell?? My phone is buzzing AGAIN. It's Andrew and I'm definitely not answering.

10:30am
It's a lazy Saturday and I only have two things on my TO DO LIST:
1. Order take-out
2. Go to Bikram yoga

5:30pm
On the way to yoga and pushing it. My belly is poking out because I've been eating all day and the class starts at six so I'm probably going to be stuck getting the hottest spot in the studio.

6:24pm
If I were one minute later, I would be on the outside of the door - looking in. But instead, I have a third row view of the front row. And there he is - no shirt, Photoshopped abs, perfect muscles and the devil's brilliant smile. His cocoa brown skin- glistening with new sweat. It's only been 20 seconds and his nickname has been reinstated - BMM is back.

8:45pm
Class is over and yes it started on a lustfully conniving foot, but the night has taken a turn. On the elevator ride down BMM suggested that we grab dinner. He said he wanted to talk and I said yes.

9:30pm
Dinner is going well, but deep down, I know that something is not right. BMM is talking and I'm listening. Again, he tells me that he's sorry about what happened earlier in the year. Again he tells me that his marriage still isn't going well and that it's going to take some time, but he wants out. And lastly he tells me that when he saw me in class today, even though we've met before, I still represent something different, something new. Again, I stop him mid-sentence and ask, "Why did you get married?" and he paused.

9:35pm
Listening to Darren fumble through the answer to the question I just asked him. And yes, he is now back to being called Darren because again I realize that there is definitely nothing sexy or rugged about this man.

9:45pm
In a cab. I left Darren at the restaurant. There were no hugs, no kisses.

10:55pm
I'm home and wide-awake. I'm writing – working on my SMART GIRLS RULES and Darren's dumb ass is the reason for the next one:

SMART GIRLS RULE #10
YOU CAN'T MARRY A MARRIED MAN.

Sunday, December 9th
11:00am
Going to the gym and then the wine store. Tonight is Ava's dinner party and I can't show up with *Two-Buck Chuck.*

3:00pm
Taking a disco nap.

5:59pm
I'm up and getting dressed. Dinner starts at eight.

8:15pm
Everyone is here and looks fabulous. Ava wanted us to get dressed up and we all obliged. Cindy and John are matching, both wearing off white, Liv and her date Aaron are doing Brooklyn Hipster, while Madelyn and Joshua are looking NYC chic, both in black leather, and Ava is wearing a red cocktail dress and her new beau, Phillip, is dapper in a grey wool suit with red tie, cuffs, and lapel pin.

8:45pm
We are seated and as the wine flows and the conversation spews, I can't but notice that the chair next to me is empty.

10:00pm
Dinner is over and now it is time to PARTY! As usual, Madelyn, Liv, and I are ready to go.

11:00pm
We are at a lounge having drinks and Joshua is still my wingman. I'm the odd girl out with no date and he's trying his best.

11:34pm
Three strikes and everyone is out. Every guy that Joshua has attempted to hook me up with has sucked and I'm going to the bathroom to fix my face because maybe it's me and not them.

11:37pm
In the bathroom and no, it's not ME. It's THEM. Madelyn and Liv joined me and both agree that I look great.

Monday, December 10th

1:05am
PARTY!! We just got to SNATCH. It's a brand new nightclub and since we are with "The Abrahams," we're carte blanche.

3:15am
Tonight was great and now all of us are going our separate ways. As Liv and her date jump in a taxi and Madelyn and Joshua get in their chauffeured car, I watch. There are plenty of cabs so it's not as if I'm left by myself, but yet as I get in the cab and shut the door, I can't help but look over and again see that the seat next to me is empty.

8:33am
At the office and Kelly isn't coming in until ten. I still have work to do, but at least I don't have to rush.

1:00pm
Going to the gym and taking a Spin class.

2:15pm
Meeting with Kelly. It's time to plan the D.E.F.I.N.I.T.I.O.N. holiday party and she wants to go over the guest list.

4:15pm
Ava just sent a text.
> ALEXA...I HOPE YOU FELT OK ABOUT LAST NIGHT. JUST KNOW THAT A DATE IS JUST THAT A DATE AND WHAT I WANT FOR YOU IS SOO MUCH MORE. YOU DESERVE A GUY THAT WILL TOTALLY FULFILL ALL OF YOUR NEEDS.
>
> BTW... YOU LOOKED AMAZING...

4:16pm
My reply:
> THANK U AVA. I NEEDED TO HEAR THIS. BTW... IM HAPPY FOR YOU. PHILLIP IS A GREAT GUY.

6:30pm
Leaving the office and going to yoga.

10:00pm
On the way uptown I received a text from Joan. She wants to meet for dinner tomorrow and of course I said yes.

11:00pm
I'm wide awake and as I flip through channels looking for something to watch, I realize that maybe I should be reading. My next book on Cindy's list is *Half of a Yellow Sun.*

11:45pm
Wow. So far this novel is a serious read. I'm only on page 23, but I want to flip ahead. I stopped and goggled the book and in the short synopsis online it

describes acts of triumph, ongoing pain, struggle, and an affair that sounds deceitfully intriguing.

Tuesday, December 11th
8:47am
Traci and I are grabbing coffee and croissants for the office. Kelly called an impromptu meeting.

9:45am
The work doesn't stop. I thought things might slow down a bit since the holiday season is approaching, but I was wrong. We have to start working on the February issue now.

12:30pm
No gym today. Working lunch.

2:59pm
I have one minute to write. Kelly wants to meet so we can go over her schedule for the next two weeks.

Tuesday at 3

"Tick-Tock"

I'm nearing the end of the rope and know it. Each decision is getting easier and taking shorter to figure out and it feels good. I'm in the best place I can be. A girl who is jumping head first into her womanhood. Learning to say never again and really mean, never again. Realizing that I'm just steps away from reaching that place in life where accepting OK is not OK. That place where "maybe" is not an option as I'm looking for the truth.

The clock is ticking and my tolerance for mediocrity, bullshit, and shortcomings is winding down.

8:30pm
Meeting Joan for dinner.

10:30pm
What an amazing dinner. The women in my life are truly
my everything. Joan is soo happy for me and I'm happy
for her. Cassandra is a perfect fit and all is well.
I invited them both to the magazine holiday party and
she promised to add it to her calendar.

Wednesday, December 12th
9:04am
At the office and today will be hectic. Not only do I
have to work with Traci to create the invite for the
party, I also have to find a venue ASAP. Kelly does not
want to host it at the office space as she thinks it
will be too small.

12:00pm
I'm on a roll. I've set up three appointments this
afternoon with potential restaurants where I can host
the party.

2:00pm
We are heading out now. My first appointment is at two-
thirty and Liv is coming with me.

3:15pm
The venue is perfect. The decor is modern, the
atmosphere is cool, and the food is good. However, it's
expensive and we have to keep looking. As bad as Liv
and I want to stay and keep drinking and eating, we
have to go. Our next appointment is at three-thirty.

3:39pm
We're late and the owner of the restaurant is pissed.

3:49pm
The owner's attitude is terrible. While he was giving
his pitch, Liv excused herself and when she returned

she stated that we had an emergency back at the office
and needed to leave.

3:55pm
On the way to the last appointment. Liv was lying about
the emergency and I knew it. The owner's attitude was
soo bad that there was no way in hell we would host
anything at his restaurant.

4:30pm
The shoe is now on the other foot. Liv and I are on
time and the event planner is late.

4:45pm
We're still waiting.

4:49pm
We're leaving. Liv insisted.

6:30pm
Back at the office. Liv went home. I came back to grab
my stuff. I'm taking an eight o'clock yoga class.

6:45pm
On my way to the subway and passing by the
Mediterranean restaurant. The owner is outside smoking
a fag and as I smile and say hi, I think to myself –
this would actually be a great place to hold the
holiday party. I'm going to approach him.

7:17pm
Clearly I'm no longer going to yoga. Demetri the owner
is excited and needs the business. The restaurant is
available. The cost to host the space is unbelievable
and he wants me to try everything on the menu.

9:15pm
Finally on the way home and my time was well spent.

10:15pm
My phone is buzzing. It's Ray and I'm not answering.

11:15pm
My phone is buzzing. It's Kola and I'm not answering.

Thursday, December 13th
12:15am
I need to go to bed, but I can't stop reading. I'm on page 49 of the book.

7:00am
My phone is buzzing. It's Andrew and I'm definitely not answering.

9:16am
Kelly gave me the green light. We're having the holiday party at the Mediterranean restaurant and she likes the eVites that Traci and I worked on.

9:29am
Grabbing coffee and pastries for the office.

12:00pm
I just hit send. The party is next Friday and I'm excited.

6:22pm
On the way to yoga and rushing. The class starts at seven.

9:00pm
On the way home. Tonight's class was stellar. No Darren sighting – just Namaste.

10:59pm
I'm home and reading.

11:09pm
Liv sent a text. Her new guy has four tickets to a play tomorrow night and the couple he invited canceled so

she wants to know if I'm interested and if my answer is yes, she wants to know if I have a guy to bring so the other ticket doesn't go to waste.

11:04pm
I replied:
> YES!! BUT – AS OF RIGHT NOW I HAVE NO DATE ☺
> BUT STRANGER SHIT HAS HAPPENED SO I'LL HIT
> U IN THE AM.

Friday, December 14th
6:30am
I'm up early. I have to grab something to wear to the play. As of right now I have no date, but again stranger shit has happened.

9:00am
At the office and my email is flooded with RSVPs. The party is going to be the bomb.

10:30am
I'm doing a coffee run. It was my suggestion only because I wanted some time to think. Who'dathunkit?? I met Kelly in January in the bathroom, both of us just being girls. Complimenting one another and, almost a year later, that encounter has changed my life.

11:30am
Popping out to drop off the deposit check and sign the contract for the D.E.F.I.N.I.T.I.O.N holiday party.

1:00pm
On the way to the gym for a quick run and as I pass Liv's office she yells out, asking if I had a date for the play. Of course I respond by nodding my head no and then again saying, "But stranger shit has happened."

7:00pm
Note: ***Stranger shit didn't happen,*** and I have no date. I'm on the way to meet Liv and her guy at the theater. She left early to go home and change.

7:59pm
The play is about to start. The lights in the theater dim and as the still excitement takes over the audience, I look over and again see that the seat next to me is empty.

11:55pm
The play was damn good and now Liv and I are starring in ACT III. We're at a restaurant/lounge downtown. Her new guy, Addison was tired and left us to our own devices.

Saturday, December 15th
3:55am
Scene: Two girls partying their asses off. Every guy in the club wants in.

4:30am
Scene: Two girls part ways. Girl #1 goes home to her man. Girl #2 goes home by herself.

10:03am
Scene: Girl #2 is lying in the bed, her hands wrapped tight around a billowing silhouette. She clutches and pulls tight, thrusting her pelvis forward, pursing her lips, moving in for a kiss. Pressing ahead, waiting to feel a soft and supple exchange but it's suddenly stopped by a bitter and bland truth. Her tongue is left feeling mildly scathed. The truth becomes apparent. She's making out with a pillow.

10:43am
I'm GIRL #2 and awake now and still clutching my new man, Mr. Pillow. It's a li'l chilly in the apartment and I need some fake body heat.

11:03am
Remarkably I'm not hung over, but not pushing my luck.
I'm hitting the corner and grabbing mashed potatoes
and Gatorade.

11:33am
ACT III (the finale)
Girl #2 is back in bed but not alone. She's found
comfort in both her mashed potatoes and Mr. Pillow.

7:31pm
ENCORE
Girls #1 and #2 are at it again. After girl talk, a
few hours of beauty rest and more mashed potatoes,
Liv and I have risen looking and feeling better than
ever. And again have been blessed by NYC and all of
HER offerings. We are on our way to meet Simon. He's
the bloke I met in London who said he would be in
the States during the holidays. He arrived today and
called. We're joining him for dinner.

Sunday, December 16th
4:00am
We are headed home and what a fun night. Simon is even
cooler now that he is on the other side of the pond.
He was a total gentleman and treated Liv and I like
the Queen. We wanted for nothing. At dinner he ordered
for us, at the nightclub he ushered us in and when it
was time for the post party eats, he stepped up to the
hostess and arranged for us to be seated without a
wait. When we finished breakfast, he put us in a taxi
and said we would do it all over again tomorrow.

11:49am
We are up and no mashed potatoes are needed. Liv awoke
with Addison on her mind and is now on her way to meet
him for brunch so she can attempt to redeem herself
from the other night and I'm going to the gym for a
quick workout and then meeting up with Simon. He wants
to go to the museum.

4:53pm
Our trip to the museum was simply lovely and I'm now back to smoking fags and speaking in my dreadful British accent. We're in a taxi heading downtown to grab an early dinner.

8:00pm
Simon is brilliant and I couldn't thank him enough. Today was *smashing, darling, smashing.* He is a lot of fun and when he makes it back to the States or when I make it back to London we both promise to reach out.

Monday, December 17th
8:30am
The RSVPs are still rolling in. The party is going to be packed.

10:55am
Meeting with Kelly in five minutes.

11:23am
My work never stops. Kelly gave me a list of her **must haves** for the party which include:

- White roses
- White tablecloths
- Delicious yet healthy passed tapas and
- A signature cocktail named the DEFINITION (of course)

12:17pm
On my way to meet Demetri to discuss the party details.

1:00pm
Back at the office. Kelly is leaving early today so no lunchtime workout.

6:00pm
Yoga time.

8:33pm
Leaving Yoga and meeting Michael. He sent a text while I was in class.

10:00pm
OMG... While at dinner, my "not boyfriend" boy-friend confessed that he was cheating on me. He has a new girlfriend and is considering marriage. I invited him and the possible "Misses" to the holiday party.

10:45pm
I'm home and my phone is buzzing. It's a text from Kola.
SEXI LEXI. WHERE R U. I WANNA C U.

11:35pm
I replied.

Tuesday, December 18th
12:15am
I'm late. I told Kola I would be there by twelve-thirty but that ain't happening. I wanted to look super pretty and went through several outfit changes. I finally decided on pretty in pink. I'm wearing blush pink skinny jeans, matching off-the-shoulder cashmere sweater, and pink fishnets. I completed the look with sleek suede pumps and leather biker jacket. I'm feeling super cute, but dipping into the bathroom for one last look before I head out the door.

12:16am
I'm in the mirror and as I continue to stare at myself I realize that I'm wasting my pretty. I've gotten all dolled up for a boy who made it clear that he's not ready to settle down. A boy who just wants to have an awesome time with me and I want a guy who is ready to spend a lifetime with me.

12:17am
Still staring in the mirror and smiling at myself. This is it. My FINALE. I'm not going out with Kola and

for that matter any guy who is not willing to be my everything. I know I've said this before, but tonight I mean it.

12:18pm
My phone is buzzing.

12:27am
I'm out of the bathroom and on the couch. I've just kicked off my pumps and my legs are stretched across the glass coffee table. I'm sending Kola a text telling him that I'm not gonna make it.

12:49am
Still on the couch. I'm eating popcorn and watching TV. I grabbed a blanket from the bed. I'm feeling pretty in pink and empowered.

7:00am
I'm up and have five missed calls and eight missed text messages. Kola is pissed and as far as he is concerned he's done with me. His last text read:

> LEXI I WAS EXPECTING U 2NITE. U LET ME DOWN I HAD DECIDED THAT WE WOULD HANG AND U DIDNT CUM THRU LEXI I WILL NEVER ASK U OUT AGAIN. ☹

7:05am
Back in the bathroom, again looking in the mirror. My smile is bright. My makeup from last night still looks good and I can't help but think about Kola's text. My Kola, well he can eat a dick. Actually he can eat jollof rice and peppa soup and that way by the time he's able to eat the dick that I'm proposing, his mouth will be soo hot that he'll die.

8:45am
Coffee run.

9:45am
Meeting with Liv to go over P.R. stuff for the party.

11:00am
Meeting with Kelly to go over her schedule.

12:45pm
Grabbing lunch for the office.

2:00pm
Compiling the guest list so I can go over it with Kelly
at three-thirty.

2:59pm
Time to write.

Tuesday at 3

"My 'Him'"

Yes, I'm in love with my newfound selfishness. Standing high on my soapbox preaching to my unconfirmed audience about womanhood. Commanding they follow in my footsteps. Pressing the importance of being in control of your journey.

And as I declare how good all of this clarity feels, I'm still secretly hoping that each of us will find our "HIM" as he will be the reason that our legs buckle. The reason our stomachs drop. He will be the guy whose infatuation never tires because it has nothing to do with outside beauty, and everything to do with HIM just wanting his "HER."

My Him...

Now that I know for sure that this is the only guy I want, I'll wait. Because I now have the courage to go without until we meet.

3:30pm
In Kelly's office and she is on fire. The printer has screwed up and the first issue of the magazine is not going to be ready by the party.

5:30pm
Working with Traci and not leaving anytime soon. Kelly, Regina, Gabrielle, and Liv left to attend a holiday party and we are pulling images from the first issue that can be blown up to poster size. If we can't have the issue to pass out, Kelly wants the best pages displayed throughout the restaurant.

9:33pm
I'm home. I grabbed take-out from the Chinese restaurant and a bottle of wine from the liquor store. I need to have fake "happy hour." I'm celebrating tonight. Being a big girl is hard. I can't pretend that I'm not still thinking about Kola; that I'm not still rehashing all of the decisions I've made this year. Some may have been stupid. Some may have been smart. But the common denominator is that they all added to my growth.

Wednesday, December 19th
8:45am
Traci and I are going to the local print shop. We selected twelve images that will be displayed at the party.

12:38pm
Going to gym.

2:00pm
Meeting with Kelly and Traci to go over our choices.

3:05pm
Working on the guest list. The RSVPs are still coming in.

275

7:23pm
Leaving the office and hoping that I make the eight o'clock yoga class.

9:30pm
Namaste. I made it.

Thursday, December 20th
8:15am
The RSVPs are still coming in and I'm nervous. If we receive fifteen more, we will be at capacity.

9:45am
We are now over capacity. Who knew that everybody would actually be available.

9:48am
Just left Kelly's office. She isn't concerned with the restaurant being flooded. This is her baby and she is happy that everyone wants to show up.

Friday, December 21st
8:00am
In the flower district picking out flowers and vases. I know Kelly requested roses, but I'm going out on a limb and adding some lilies, tulips, and greenery. I've never fallen out of love with flowers and know that these arrangements will be perfect.

9:00am
At the office dropping off the flowers then going to the print shop.

10:00am
At the office and dropping of the prints then going to the art supply store to get easels.

10:45am
At the office and Kelly just arrived. She's given her
nod and is all smiles. We are having a quick meeting to
go over the party details.

12:00pm
Kelly told us all to leave and go and get ready for
this evening, but both Traci and I brought our clothes;
so she's going to stay and help me bring everything
over to the restaurant.

3:00pm
Time to go. The party starts at five-thirty and we want
to take our time setting up.

4:30pm
We're done! Everything is perfect.

4:59pm
It's the quiet before the storm and Traci and I are
breathing in the last minutes of calm. Demetri made us
a sample plate. We figured we would eat now since Kelly
will be relying on us to play hostess.

5:02pm
Kelly just sent Traci a text telling her that she was
on her way, so I have ten minutes to fix my face and
then it's go time.

5:12pm
Kelly is here.

5:14pm
Kelly is simultaneously nodding while saying, "I love
it. Good job."

5:19pm
The first guests have arrived, early no doubt and as Traci greets them, Kelly grabs my arm and pulls me aside.

5:24pm
Four more guests just walked in and I'm screwed. I tried to hold back my tear, but it fell and I have no time to go to the bathroom and fix my face. Kelly offered me another job. I will no longer be her assistant. In the next few months she wants me to transition out of that role and move into full time contributing writer for the magazine.

6:27pm
The restaurant is tittering on being packed, the signature cocktail is a hit and the servers can't keep the appetizer plates full.

6:45pm
We're at capacity and as I greet guests, Kelly and I lock eyes. She smiles and again mouths, "Good job."

6:46pm
It's official. We're beyond capacity and I'm sure the fire department is on the way.

7:11pm
Houston we have a problem. I spot Liv and she is getting touchy-feely with one of the investors. She looks up, smiles, and waves at me to come over. Her eyes are glossy and I know this is not good. I can tell that she's tipsy.

7:15pm
Oh Lord. She's not tipsy; she's hammered and just dropped her drink.

7:20pm
Ay Dios Mio. As she excused herself and headed toward the bathroom, she knocked one of the easels down.

7:26pm
Kelly and I lock eyes again and this time, she's not smiling. She mouths, "She's done." I know what this means. Operation Get Liv Outta Here is in full effect.

7:30pm
Traci will accompany Liv home and I will stay. The party is over in thirty minutes.

8:11pm
The party is winding down and even though we had a small debacle with Liv, tonight was a success and a prelude to what will be a great new year. Kelly was thrilled and wants all of us to meet at the office tomorrow at noon.

8:17pm
Traci came back and we are going to hang around and have a few drinks with Demetri and then swing by to check on Liv.

8:45pm
Leaving now and bringing Liv food. We called and she's sobered up and hungry.

Saturday, December 22nd
11:35am
We all made it to the office before noon, Liv included.

11:51pm
Again, my arm has been grabbed and I've been pulled into the corner. This time it's Liv. She wants the truth. When we dropped of food at her place, we didn't get a chance to talk. She's disappointed with herself and is nervous. She knows that her behavior was unacceptable and needs me to spill the truth.

11:56am
There wasn't too much to say besides calling out the obvious. She was plastered. Tore up from the floor up.

Loosey goosey. But as we talked, I reassured her that Kelly has her back. She is going to be just fine, and as we continue to gab, the next SGR pops in my head:

SMART GIRL RULE #11
NEVER BE THE GIRL
AT THE BOTTOM OF THE GLASS

12:13pm
Kelly is holding court. She thought the party was both sexy and savvy. She is still on cloud nine, but in between gushing about the future of the magazine, and informing us that we don't need to return to the office until January 3rd, she is subtly tearing into Liv about her behavior.

12:35pm
Kelly is done. She's excused herself, requesting that we give her five.

12:40pm
She's back and donning a Santa hat and bearing gifts. She's passing out shopping bags and we've all been instructed not to open our presents until Christmas day.

1:56pm
Kelly aka Mrs. Claus has upped the ante and is now passing out bottles of champagne.

2:25pm
A few bottles have been popped and we've all indulged, Liv included, but we have no snacks and we need to nosh. I called Demetri and he has a table for six waiting for us. We're going to have brunch at the restaurant.

4:05pm
Brunch was fun and Liv is back! She was invited to another holiday party and wants me to come. We are going to meet back up at nine.

280

11:00pm
Liv jumped back into the deep end too soon and I'm crashing at her place so I can play nurse. She had one drink too many and did a repeat of last night.

Sunday, December 23rd
11:00am
We're up and wasting no time getting out the door. Cindy has invited all of us to her house for Christmas brunch so that means we have to get gifts for everybody. This will be Miss Harlow's first Christmas and she's going all out.

5:00pm
We're done and wasting no time getting out of the store. We are starving and need to eat now.

8:30pm
Of course dinner turned into drinks. We ended up going to a cool place in Soho and met some guys, but we keep it easy. Both Liv and I only had one cocktail. We agreed to both go home and rest as we have more shopping to do in the morning, not to mention that we'll be attending nonstop parties from now until New Year's Eve.

Monday, December 24th
10:00am
I'm up and meeting Liv at noon. I'm going to head out to grab her gift now and then we'll meet so we can pick up our last few presents.

4:00pm
While we were out shopping, Madelyn sent a text. One of Joshua's teammates is having a Christmas Eve party at his loft in Tribeca. I sent Ava a text and she's coming with Phillip. I called Cassandra and she's in too. I'm going to meet her at her place and then we'll swing by and pick up Liv.

Tuesday, December 25th
12:01am
Merry Christmas!!

12:15am
Forget the shopping we did yesterday and today, the best gifts are here. From the minute we arrived, the three of us have continuously been swept off our feet. The guys tonight are handsome, charming and totally cool.

11:17am
The three of us will surely have coal in our stockings. We stayed up all night and have to be at Cindy's by one o'clock and this would be fine if each of us were at home, but none of us are. One of Joshua's teammates was staying at a hotel very close to the loft and got a room for Cassandra and I. And Liv — Ms. Liv. She just sent a text. She's going to meet us at Cindy's apartment. After the champagne toast, she left the party with her latest catch.

1:13pm
We all made it, Liv included. Cindy's apartment is a winter wonderland and baby Harlow looks like an angel.

2:30pm
It's time to open presents!

2:52pm
It's my turn and I'm opening Kelly's present first because I'm dying to know what it is. I begin to tear the paper and Cindy yells out, "My God, Alexa have some dignity and read the card first." I smile and then read aloud:

Alexa, timing is everything and this is your time.

2:54pm
Inside the immaculately wrapped box, underneath mounds of silver metallic tissue is a copy of the first issue

of D.E.F.I.N.I.T.I.O.N magazine and in true Alexa form, I pull it out and flip to page 46. And there it is - my column. I'm doing my best to hold in my tears, but can't.

2:56pm
The girls all join in for a hug.

2:59pm
It was a quick cry and now I'm inspired. I yell out to Cindy to pass me a pen. I un-crumple the wrapping paper. It's time to write.

Tuesday at 3

Smart Girl Rule #12

Cherish Your Journey

This is the final rule.

Wednesday, December 26th
2:00pm
Detoxing today. I'm going to just chill at home and later go to yoga and then come back home and chill some more. The *Accessory Magazine* party is tomorrow and Kelly wants us all to be there.

Thursday, December 27th
7:00pm
The party is nice, but there's no Helga. I guess my horoscope, my future, is really up to me.

Friday, December 28th
10:00am
Morning detox, then yoga, and then another party.

Saturday, December 29th
2:32pm
Afternoon detox, then yoga, and then another party.

Sunday, December 30th
3:00pm
All day detox. Tomorrow is New Year's Eve and I want to look and feel good.

Monday, December 31st
11:00am
Meeting Ava, Madelyn, Cindy, Liv, Cassandra, and Kelly at the nail salon for a mani/pedi.

4:00pm
I'm home. After the nail salon we all went shopping. Tonight is going to be fun. We're going to the hottest party in town. Of course Joshua and Madelyn were invited by the host and the other host just happened to be a client of Ava's firm. Thus the stars continue to align, and it turns out that the party planner is Kelly's sorority sister. Thus, that left three plus ones that went to myself, Liv, and Cassandra.

11:00pm
We're all here looking and feeling fabulous.

11:59pm
Champagne glasses are all held high and it's time to count down. Ten, Nine, Eight, Seven, Six, Five, Four, Three, Two, One…

Tuesday, January 1, 2013
12:00am
Happy New Year!

12:01am
It's been one minute and the stroke of midnight hasn't made a bit of difference. The "ball drop" didn't mean shit. All of the confetti and streamers, champagne and smiling faces – I need none of it to validate my joy. Last year I received the best present and learned the most important lesson.

I found my Womanhood.

2:59pm
It's time to write.

Tuesday at 3
THE END

3:01pm

My phone is ringing and I know the number. It's Steven. The boy who was never going to give me what I wanted. The boy that I asked, that I begged because I wanted to get married, but he didn't. So as I stare down at my phone, I wonder, *What could he possibly want?*

SMART GIRL RULES

#1 OWN YOUR WOMANHOOD
#2 NEVER CRY AT THE OFFICE
#3 TRY TO ALWAYS LOOK NICE
#4 GET YOUR ROCKS OFF DURING FOREPLAY
#5 ALWAYS KEEP SUNGLASSES IN YOUR HANDBAG
#6 BE A SMART GIRL
#7 NEVER BE THE PENCIL IN BITCH
#8 PICK YOUR LAST DAY TO CRY
#9 NO MORE FREE BJ'S
#10 YOU CAN'T MARRY A MARRIED MAN
#11 NEVER BE THE GIRL AT THE BOTTOM OF THE GLASS
#12 CHERISH YOUR JOURNEY

Printed in the United States
By Bookmasters

04068938-00800893